MY BIG MOUTH

10 Songs I Wrote That Almost Got Me Killed

For Dru

Copyright © 2011 by Peter Hannan

Library of Congress Cataloging-in-Publication Data

Hannan, Peter.
My big mouth : 10 songs I wrote that almost got me killed / by Peter Hannan.
p. cm.
Summary: When Davis Delaware moves to a new school after the death of his mother, he immediately gets on the wrong side of Gerald, the school bully, when he creates a band called The Amazing Dweebs along with Molly, the girl he has a crush on—who also happens to be Gerald's girlfriend.
ISBN 978-0-545-16210-4
[1. Rock groups—Fiction. 2. Interpersonal relations—Fiction. 3. Bullies—Fiction. 4. High schools—Fiction. 5. Schools—Fiction.] I. Title.
PZ7.H1978My 2011
[Fic]—dc22
2010034426

10 9 8 7 6 5 4 3 2 1   11 12 13 14 15

Printed in the U.S.A.   23
First printing, July 2011
Book design by Chris Stengel

Peter Hannan

MY BIG MOUTH

10 Songs I Wrote That Almost Got Me Killed

Scholastic Press
New York

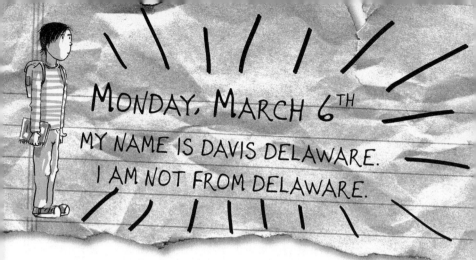

MONDAY, MARCH 6TH
MY NAME IS DAVIS DELAWARE.
I AM NOT FROM DELAWARE.

Everybody knows why guys start bands: to get girls. But that's not why I started the Amazing Dweebs. I did it for one girl. I had no clue that girls and bands were such a dangerous combination.

I saw Molly coming down the hall that Monday, the very first time I stepped into Woodrow Wilson High. I found out her name almost instantly because people kept saying it: *Hi, Molly. Where are you going, Molly? WAIT UP, MOLLY!*

I transferred schools in ninth grade late that year. Really late . . . one month before spring break. Thanks a lot, Pops. He said it would be better to meet some kids to hang out with during the summer than to wait until fall. Yeah, right. We both knew it was just because of when his new job started. My mom had died the year before, so we were trying to start a whole new life: new house, new school, new town. Except it felt like the same old life. Only worse. We'd moved eighty-seven miles, from one crappy school to another.

It was at the very moment I saw Molly that I finally understood what the whole girl thing was about. I mean, it's not like I didn't have a clue before. There had been lots of clues. But now they all added up to Molly. The way she walked, the way she talked, everything about the way she just *was*: reddish hair, not too neat, not too messy; tons of freckles — some people don't like freckles, but those are people we call tons of stupid; black Converse; and a skirt. Pretty, a little tomboyish, but smiling, laughing, funny, a lot of attitude. What a girl.

And get this: She was wearing a Mad Manny the Monkey T-shirt. Mad Manny was the mascot for a chain of stores called Guitar Jungle. They had a series of insane TV commercials that were super-surreal. Each was totally low budget and bizarre in its own way. But they all ended with a guy in a monkey suit swinging in on a vine, playing an electric guitar and howling, "This is Mad Manny the Monkey saying, 'Swing on down to Guitar Jungle. Our prices will drive you bananas!'" And then he would crash off camera, making a gigantic racket of breaking glass, followed by wild monkey chatter. Mad Manny was mad-angry, mad-crazy, and mad-cool. A so-bad-it's-good kind of thing. The ads were a litmus test. Most people hated them. If you loved them, you were okay in my book.

Molly was way beyond okay. She was in a much better book, on a much higher shelf. I knew instantly that I would never — could never — talk to her. You probably think I couldn't know that from way down the hall, but believe me, it was obvious. I *saw her* . . . and I *knew me*. She disappeared down another corridor and I stared at the spot where she'd been standing.

BLAM! My trance was broken by the unmistakable flesh-on-metal slam, rattle, and *owww* of a student/locker collision. I turned in time to see a huge kid

towering over a small kid who was lying on the floor. Actually, it was hard to determine the size of that kid because he was curled up into a ball.

He was rocking and moaning in a way that seemed to say, *Okay, you hurt me. Now please leave me to my misery.*

But Gorilla Dude wasn't satisfied. He faked like he was going to punch the little guy in the head.

The kid flinched and instantly started to cry. "Don't hit me . . . don't hit me . . . don't hit me . . ."

Bingo. Big goon got what he wanted.

He laughed and strolled down the hallway in my direction. He was like a bully from central casting . . . the muscles, the swagger, the smirk. Didn't he realize he was a walking cliché? Don't these idiots see movies or watch TV? I was almost embarrassed for him.

Totally terrified of him, too, of course.

Cliché or not, there will always be boneheads who want to be bullies. Unfortunately, the bully thing works.

Just then, a funny little lady popped out of the school office and waved to me. She didn't even notice the crime scene to her left. By then, the victim was on his knees, digging through his locker and pretending that nothing had happened. (The tormented typically helps the tormentor cover up the crime.)

The huge bully kid walked toward the lady and

greeted her like they were best friends.

"Hi, Mrs. Toople," he said, smiling and waving as he passed her. "Hope you're having a great Monday."

"Oh, you, too, Gerald!" she said in a falsetto that made me think of a man trying to sound like a lady. "Monday is my favorite day of the week!" She approached me. "Davis, I presume?"

"You presume right."

Her smile got even bigger. Wow. She was unbelievably enthusiastic. "Hi, I'm Mrs. Toople, the office coordinator! How are you today?"

"Monday is my favorite day of the week," I said.

"Mine, too!" she chirped, missing my sarcasm. "Here's your locker number and combination!" She handed me a few sheets of paper. "And your class schedule. Follow me!"

She turned and almost crashed into the principal.

"Oops!" said Toople. "Excuse us, Mr. Rigo! Meet Davis . . . This is his very first day!"

"Right," Mr. Rigo said, putting his hand on my shoulder. "I remember chatting with your dad. So, how was the move?" He had to know that my mom died. The hand-on-the-shoulder thing was a total tip-off.

"Good, good," I stammered.

"Well, 'good-good' is twice as good as 'good,'" he said, glancing at the hall clock. "Okay, I have a conference to get to, so you have a good-good first day. You, too, Mrs. Toople."

"All righty! All righty!" said Mrs. Toople.

Was she high on happy pills?

She continued cheerfully, leading me down the hall. "Over there's the nearest boys' room, and there are more around the school of course, so, you know, if you need one, we have them. Well, of course we have them. And here's the gym. Never met a boy who didn't like gym!"

She hadn't met me.

Mrs. Toople dropped me off at my first class ever at Woodrow Wilson: first-period English. She cracked open the door and sang out, "Knock, knock! Hellooo? Miss Danderbrook?"

Miss Danderbrook was standing up front, addressing thirty-odd half-asleep students. She froze in mid-sentence, her index finger in the air. Then she turned to us, mouth open wide . . . silent.

"Miss Danderbrook, students," said Toople, "say hello to Davis, the new boy from Delaware!"

"Actually," I said, "I'm not *from* Delaware . . ."

But nobody heard that, because they were whining in that super-bored voice all students use when asked to repeat something back like kindergar-teners: "Helll-llllo, Day-visssssss . . ."

Danderbrook was tall and thin, prob-ably about my dad's age, but she seemed older because of what she was wearing. It was your basic English teacher/librarian uniform: cardigan sweater, white button-down blouse, skirt below the knee, and—here's the kicker—glasses with that chain around the neck. Those are pretty much the universal symbol for *I think I'm smart and I know I'm old.*

"We're taking a test today, Davis," she said, "but since you obviously haven't done the read-ing, you can just take a seat and make yourself comfort-able for the next forty minutes."

Comfortable, right. No problem. Except that I have never been comfortable in my entire life. I tend to be on the nervous side. I fidget. I drum my fingers on tabletops, wiggle my toes in my shoes, and doodle constantly.

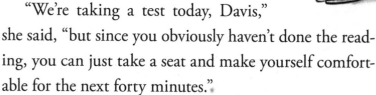

There was one empty seat toward the back of the room and I headed for it, avoiding eye contact. I sat

THE END

down, pulled out my notebook, and drew a picture of a dog floating in midair above a pond stocked with piranhas. The dog's eyes were bugging out, his teeth chattering. He looked like the most flustered, freaked-out critter on Earth.

The dog was definitely me.

I filled up three or four more pages with drawings, scribbles, and odd thoughts. I drew a very unflattering picture of Danderbrook, not because I had anything against her, but just because she was, you know, a teacher.

The bell rang and everyone groaned. I closed my notebook.

"Okay, people," said Danderbrook, "hand them over."

Everyone groaned again as they stood up. It was only then that I noticed that Molly was in the class and had been sitting a couple of desks back the whole time. I couldn't believe it. I had assumed she was a junior, or at least a sophomore. I guess that's why Mom always said I should keep my head up—I might see something worth seeing. She also said that I needed to forget my nervousness and talk to people. But thinking about that just made me a lot more nervous. What would I say to a girl like Molly? *Nice shirt, I love Mad Manny the Monkey, too*? It sounded so creepy and random, like a sleazy pickup line. Molly had no idea who I was.

She walked right by me, and I thought of my mom again. She would want me to try.

So, I panicked and attempted to say something . . . but then changed my mind.

My mouth has a slower turn-off switch than my brain, so a small, birdlike squawk came out. It was a ridiculous sound. Someone hearing it would either think I was mentally deficient or just totally wacko. Molly didn't turn around or anything, so I figured maybe she didn't hear. Thank god. She handed her test to Danderbrook and headed into the hallway, instantly surrounded by girls.

She was like the nucleus of an atom; her friends buzzed around her like electrons. I couldn't help thinking that she looked a little bored by the attention. Almost like she had been popular for so long, she was tired of it and wanted to be something else. But she didn't look mean or impatient or anything. That was the thing—she didn't seem stuck-up, like most popular girls.

THE END

For the rest of the day, I was on the lookout for Molly. I went about my business—first, to my locker. The combination worked fine, but the door jammed and when I yanked on it, it unstuck, rattled loudly, and whacked me in the knee.

"Oww," I said to myself, teeth clenched like a ventriloquist, hoping no one had witnessed my little spaz attack.

Then to biology, lunch, Spanish. I met teachers, other students. But I remember almost nothing about all that. It turned out that Molly wasn't in any of my other classes, so all that sticks out are a few TMMs: Tiny Molly Moments.

9:42 AM:
Walking down the hall, the back of her head bobbing for a moment in a sea of bored humanity before vanishing again.
11:16 AM:
Through the window in math class, Molly in gym shorts, walking outside in a line of girls with field-hockey sticks.
Lunch:
Molly sitting with friends. Me sitting alone.

1:53 PM:
Passing by the doorway of a classroom, Molly's high-tops on the ends of her perfect legs, stretched out in front of her desk.

When I got home that afternoon, I started my homework. After a while, Dad arrived with Chinese takeout. We sat down on the couch and loaded up our plates. Dad flipped on the TV. He never missed the news, even though he complained all the way through it.

A commercial was on, so he turned to me and asked, "How'd your first day go?"

"It went."

"Did you meet anyone?"

"Nope, not really." I stabbed a piece of kung pao chicken with my fork.

"You can't name one person you met?"

"Okay, okay . . . Molly."

"Good, that's a start. Molly. Is this a *friend* friend, or *more* than a friend?"

"A non-friend." Luckily, the news started up again.

We ate and watched, and every single thing about the broadcast irritated Dad. "You can fool ninety-nine point nine percent of the people ninety-nine point nine percent of the time. Remember that."

"How could I forget?" I said. "You say it every night."

We chewed chow mein in silence.

"Five times a week, tops," he replied.

TUESDAY, MARCH 7TH
THE BUTCHER

The next day, I arrived at school, dumped my stuff in my locker — which stuck again, *owww* — and headed for Danderbrook's room. I was determined to say hello to Molly, only this time not in Insane Bird-ese.

But when I got there, Molly wasn't at her desk.

The bell rang. Still no Molly.

"Edwin," said Danderbrook, "would you kindly bring Molly her homework? She has a student council off-site today."

"No problem," said a short kid with thick glasses and hair that almost totally covered them. He looked even smaller because he slouched down low in his chair, eyes just barely peering over the desktop. He talked out of the side of his mouth like a gangster in an old movie or something. "Her house is only two and a half miles out of my way. If I walk four miles an hour, the typical speed of a typical human — even though I'm far from typical — that would rob me of merely thirty-seven and

13

THE END

a half minutes of my life. No big deal. I certainly have nothing better to do with my time."

But Danderbrook didn't even raise an eyebrow. "That's enough, Edwin."

Really. What was this kid's problem? He was apparently deeply in love with the sound of his own voice.

Sure enough, after class in the hallway, Edwin was *still* talking, even though he was alone. I was walking along near him and eventually realized that his chatter was for my benefit. He didn't look at me, just kept running off at the mouth, making sure I was the only one to hear.

"Oh, wonderful," he said. "Look what we have here, the Prince of Dunceness himself."

Up ahead, Gerald was leaning against the wall, hand cupped to his mouth like a megaphone. He chanted in a low, frog-like voice, in rhythm with Edwin's steps: "Dweeb, dweeb, dweebity, dweeb . . ."

It seemed like Edwin was used to it. He pretended not to notice. Instead, he just murmured under his breath.

"Dunce, dunce, dunce-ity, dunce . . ."

"Who is this Gerald joker, anyway?" I said softly to Edwin. "Isn't he embarrassed to be such a *typical* bonehead?"

"You give him too much credit," Edwin replied, still not looking at me as he talked. And talked. It felt like the kind of secret conversation two inmates have in a prison yard.

"He actually thinks he's special . . . the one and only Gerald Boggs. But he hates the name Gerald, which is why  he has so many nicknames: Big G, G-Man, and his favorite, the Butcher. *My* favorite is Gerald the Idiot Turd-faced Baboon. Okay, I made that one up. The Butcher is all-county quarterback, all-state wrestler, and all-galaxy fool. He is also the leader of a moronic band called the Butchers. Clever—his name is 'the Butcher' and the band is called 'the Butchers.' Couldn't it at least be 'Butcher and the Cuts of Meat' or something? Anyway, his family is rolling in dough, so he isn't just a jerk—he's a spoiled-rotten-rich jerk. The worst kind."

"Got it," I said.

Gym was next, so I stopped at my locker to grab my gym clothes. Edwin kept walking. He didn't even say

good-bye or anything. Zero eye contact.

My locker stuck again, but this time I avoided banging my knee. I stood there and watched Gerald for a minute from behind my locker door. He seemed a lot older. He had a mustache, and not a peach-fuzz one, either. He was probably born with it. I could totally see him sucking on a baby bottle with that hairy lip. He traveled with a small pack of psychopaths. They walked in wedge formation, parting the hallway crowd like the Red Sea.

The bell rang and the hall was instantly deserted. I grabbed my gym clothes, slammed my locker door, and took off.

"Yoo-hoo! No running, Davis!" chirped a familiar voice. "Maybe running is allowed in·those Delaware schools, but not here," Mrs. Toople continued.

"Actually, running is required in all Delaware hallways," I said. "But today I'm just late."

"No excuse," she said, unfazed. "The policy is for your own safety, dear."

Please, please, please don't call me 'dear,' I thought. *I didn't even let my mother call me 'dear.'*

I walked slowly until I turned the corner, then broke into a sprint again. But I came to a dead end where I thought the gym was.

Edwin emerged from a bathroom. "Hey, it's the

new kid . . . the *lost* new kid," he said. "What's the matter? Lose your compass? You can wander aimlessly for the rest of your life, or you can ask somebody. Me, for instance."

"Locker room?" I kept it short and sweet. Unlike some people I knew.

"You're more lost than I thought," he said, pulling  out a wad of hall passes, all signed and rolled up like paper money. "First of all, you'll need this. Go that way, take a left, all the way down, through the breezeway, and another left. The good news is, you'll be there."

"What's the bad news?" I asked.

"You'll be there," said Edwin, heading in the opposite direction. "Maybe leave some breadcrumbs for the return trip."

"Thanks, Mr. Hansel-and-Gretel," I said.

The locker room was totally empty when I got there, except for a heavy dose of body odor hanging in a cloud of steam. I unrolled my gym clothes. Where the heck

were my jockstrap and white socks? I'd just had them in my hand! But there was no time to go back and get them. I couldn't find an empty gym locker, so I threw on my shorts and T-shirt, stuffed my regular shirt into my pants, balled them up, and ditched them in a corner that was obviously teeming with fungus. Then I realized that my socks were an unmatching set. One black, one bright blue. Great.

I ran into the gym—and into the gym teacher. Literally. It was like running into a building. I fell flat on my back. He looked around, pretending not to notice me lying at his feet.

"What hit me? A gnat? A newt?" This got a laugh. Then he looked down. "Nice socks, new kid. Bet you have a pair just like 'em at home."

Good one. Clever.

"Yes," I said, handing him my hall pass. "I'm Davis Delaware."

"*Yes, sir* or *Yes, Mr. Shettle*," he said, crumpling the paper and throwing it in the general direction of his office. *Mr. Shettle?* I

wondered what kids called him behind his back. "And next time, wear white socks, or you'll run laps forever." This whole white-sock obsession was the telltale sign of a hard-nosed, old-school, super-jock gym teacher. In other words, a muscle-headed bureaucrat, concerned more with arbitrary rules and regulations than actual, you know, life.

He stuck a whistle in his mouth and blew hard. That's when I realized that I was standing in the middle of the court. Two dodgeball teams were lined up on opposite sides of me. I covered my face, and about a hundred balls came flying from all directions. At least half of them hit me.

I thought it was over, but when I lowered my hands, there was the Butcher. He was barreling toward me, arm cocked, ready to fire. He roared like the half man, half beast he was, and heaved the ball at approximately the speed of light.

I put my arms up again, but he'd aimed lower. *Kablam-o*, in the you-know-whats.

I doubled over and fell sideways, crashing down hard on my elbow.

"AAHHH!" I gasped. "Funny bone!" Amazingly, this *kablam-o* almost made me forget about the original *kablam-o*.

"Nice one, Delaware," said Shettle with a smile. He seemed to enjoy my pain. I crawled to the sidelines.

Edwin wandered in and sat down next to me. Through my misery, I couldn't help thinking it was weird that he didn't mention he was in this gym class when I saw him in the hall. He seemed to roam freely about the school. He hadn't even used one of those hall passes.

"You did not land on the funny bone," he said, "because it's not even a bone. It's not really that funny, either, but that's beside the point. It's actually the ulnar nerve, which passes down the arm, behind the elbow. And since there's zero fat there, it's extremely vulnerable. Bad design, really. Mother Nature probably should have gone back to the drawing board on that one. Do you feel a tingling all the way down to your pinkie?"

I flexed my hand. "How'd you know?"

"See, that's because it's a nerve, not a bone," Edwin said, nodding matter-of-factly. "There are a lot of misnomers out there. A peanut is not a nut, a silverfish is not a fish . . ."

"*Talking a lot is not necessarily saying anything*," I said pointedly.

"Headcheese is not cheese," he said, not taking the hint.

"Edwin?"

"Uh-huh?"

"Shut up."

I wasn't in the habit of telling someone I'd just met

to shut up, but Edwin didn't even seem to notice. Like it happened so often, it didn't faze him.

"And how about the sea cow?" he asked. "First of all, they've been extinct for two hundred and fifty years, but even if you could time travel, you'd find the sea cow to be nothing like a cow. More like a ten-ton mountain of floating blubber."

"Thanks for the lecture," I said.

"I've barely scratched the surface."

Edwin was not only a motormouth — he was a last-word freak.

Meanwhile, the Butcher was working the dodgeball court like an assassin. He caught five balls straight and then held them in a row against the side of his body with his left arm, like bullets in an ammo belt. There were five kids left on the other team, and he quickly picked off two. He was like a superstar athlete competing against babies.

One of the remaining targets tried to sneak off the court nonchalantly. The Butcher spotted him and spun around, dropping one of the balls in the process. The sneaking kid laughed, but the Butcher kicked the ball hard on the bounce, thwacking him in the back of the neck and knocking him down.

"He's outta there!" the Butcher roared.

"What?" I muttered. "Kicking is totally illegal in dodgeball."

"Maybe in Delaware," snarled Shettle, who was standing right behind me. "Boggs developed the foot technique last year. We call it *extreme* dodgeball."

Are you kidding me? Developed the technique? You mean, cheated?

Shettle was apparently a rules-and-regulations guy who changed the rules and regulations to suit his purposes.

The final two kids on the opposite team scuttled around like panicked cockroaches. The Butcher gripped a ball in each hand and moved to the center line. Suddenly, both insect-boys zigged when they should have zagged, crashed into each other, and collapsed right in front of him.

A normal, non-psycho jock might have tapped them out gently. But not the Butcher. He lifted both balls above his head and spiked them downward at point-

blank range with a gesture that looked like Zeus hurling twin lightning bolts from Mount Olympus. Both hit their targets: the insect-boys' heads.

They survived, but just barely.

Extreme dodgeball. Yippee.

Shettle smiled and blew his

whistle. "Okay, people," he said. "Back onto the court for round two. As soon as you're out, you can hit the showers."

Shettle pointed at me, directing me to the side opposite Gerald. Edwin didn't budge. He just sat and watched. Actually, he wasn't even watching. He was reading. That kid seemed to live by different rules.

I decided to at least try this time. I grabbed a ball and positioned myself way in the back, out of the line of fire. I figured I'd throw a kid or two out, then take a soft one and get the heck off the court.

Shettle blew the whistle and balls started flying. I picked out a kid to aim for. Not too small (I wouldn't hurt him) and not too big (he wouldn't hurt me) . . . just right. I took two steps toward him and let it fly. He ducked, and the ball skimmed the top of his head and kept going.

It smacked the Butcher right between the eyes, making a loud *ping*.

"OWWW!" His roar echoed through the gym.

Okay, that was unfortunate. Causing the Butcher to yell *owww* had to be one of the stupider accomplishments of my life. His nose got red instantly—I immediately thought of Rudolph but decided not to mention it—but he wasn't "out" since the ball had hit him on the ricochet. He spun around, looking for a loose ball to grab. But I didn't wait. I saw a ball coming and dived into its path, intentionally getting myself knocked out. Success—for now, anyway.

I turned to leave and heard a loud *ping-PING*! A ball whizzed by my head, just grazing a hair or two, bounced off the wall, and careened across the gym. It had obviously been dropkicked by the Butcher. In extreme dodgeball, even players who are already out are fair game.

I ducked into the locker room, got dressed, and walked quickly to my next class: math.

BLAH

Mr. Kirbin, the math teacher, was math-ish, therefore snooze-ish. Another forty minutes I'd never get back.

The rest of the day was more of the same. Lunch: blah. History: ancient blah. Spanish: el blah, la blah, los blahs. No Molly. No meaningful contact with intelligent life. Day two would be in the can after one last stop at my locker.

But on my way there, I noticed a commotion up ahead. People were totally cracking up. I got some funny looks, and at first I thought they were just trying to include me in the hilarity—you know, a let's-make-the-new-kid-feel-at-home kind of thing.

But then one of my missing white socks came flying from the crowd and hit me on the side of the head. The other one got me in the face. Then I saw what everyone was really laughing about. I had been in such a hurry to get to gym class, not only had I dropped my socks, I'd slammed my jockstrap in my locker door. I thought about just walking by, pretending it wasn't mine, but then I saw the handwritten letters on the elastic waistband: "DELAWARE." Mom had labeled all my gym clothes.

It was hanging there at eye level like a sad, embarrassing, personalized white flag. Surrender.

I walked up to the locker and tried to yank it out, but it was really stuck. It just stretched way out like a slingshot. This was apparently really hilarious, too, because a few assorted guffaws erupted in the hallway. But then it got quiet. Really quiet.

The crowd parted — and there stood the Butcher.

"I like what you've done with the place, dweeb," he said.

"Yeah, well, it's the attention to detail that makes all the difference," I said, trying to hide my nervousness.

It felt like the entire student population had stopped to watch. I stood in front of the locker to try to keep everyone from seeing my combination, quickly turning the dial and yanking up on the latch. It didn't budge.

Okay, this was uncomfortable.

"Nice toss in gym, too," the Butcher snarled. He moved closer, really in my face now.

"What can I tell you?" I said. "It's all in the wrist."

"Oh, Davis!" chirped Mrs. Toople, waddling out of the office like a happy duck. "I see you've met Gerald! That's neat. You two probably have a lot in common."

A lot in common? I had nothing in common with that lobotomized gorilla.

"Yes, Mrs. Toople," said Gerald in his talking-to-an-adult voice. "The new kid and I have really hit it off, haven't we, new kid?" With that, he casually walked away with a few of his goons.

I nodded as I worked through the combination again, slower this time. Success, thank god. I pulled really hard on the door to make sure it would unstick, and it flew open and banged loudly against the adjoining locker. In one quick motion, I threw the jockstrap, socks, and shorts inside, and slammed it shut again.

"Okay," I said to anybody who might still be watching. "Move along, folks. Nothing to see here."

I followed my own good advice and moved along down the hall, out the door, and headed home.

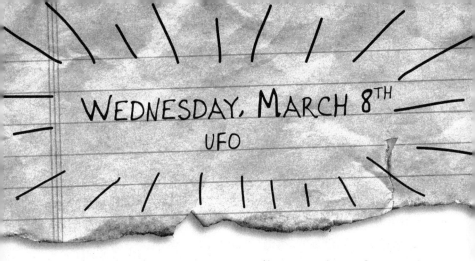

WEDNESDAY, MARCH 8TH
UFO

The next day, I was sitting alone in the cafeteria, doodling in my notebook. Ever since I can remember, I've used notebooks to draw and write in. I pretty much empty my brain into them. And ever since I started playing the guitar a couple years ago, the words have taken the form of songs. Not for anyone else, just songs I sing for myself in my room. Secret drawings, secret songs.

I wrote the first one when I was little. Actually, it was a rewrite:

Happy Burpday, you poo,
Happy Burpday, you poo,
Happy Burpday, dear (fill in the blank. The next-
    door-neighbor kid's name worked nicely),
Happy Burpday, you poo!

Mom loved it until she realized it wasn't about Winnie-the-Pooh. My dad and grandmother weren't too thrilled, either. I spent the rest of the weekend in my room. Years later, I still remembered how Mom had liked that idiotic song at first. Even though she got mad, she kind of appreciated it.

I've done my share of scribbling all over the inside of schoolbooks, too—you know, the typical zombification of presidents and other historical figures by erasing their eyeballs, blackening their teeth, adding stitches and fangs, blood and boogers. I've made flip-book movies in the margins of those really fat paperback textbooks, fat enough to really get an epic going—worms crawling over razor blades and getting sliced into segments, babies projectile-vomiting, certain people's heads popping off and bouncing along the page. Harmless fun, but fun that can get you into trouble. The teachers freak out and they freak the parents out—the freak-out domino theory. I've had actual sketchbooks, too, but the beauty of a notebook is you can pretend to be doing schoolwork while you're actually drawing pictures of your teachers as disgusting monsters or trolls or aliens or worse.

Anyway, I was scribbling away in the cafeteria while poking at a UFO (Uneatable Food-ish Object) with my fork. Just then, another UFO splatted me in the back of the neck.

What the what?

No big surprise—new kids might as well have huge targets painted on them.

You might think that I wondered who threw it, but I didn't. I knew. I squeegeed off the UFO with my hand as I turned and looked across the room.

Yup, there they were: the Goons of the Round Table.

Nothing King Arthur-ish about them, just a bunch of goons sitting together at a table that happened to be round. Every school has one spot where all the biggest, meanest idiots gather. They do everything in a pack, including throwing disgusting food-ish substances at people. And as always, in the middle of this pack sits the alpha goon, the biggest, meanest moron of the bunch, the perfect blend of creepiness and charisma.

You guessed it: Gerald "the Butcher" Boggs.

GERALD'S GAME

It was obvious what Gerald's game was. Simple, really: making kids feel bad, freak out, and cry . . . and then laughing at them. Fun. He could make some kids bawl just by evil-eyeing them from across the room.

I'd already witnessed him doing the hair-smooth move, where you jerk your hand up in a threatening way to get someone to flinch—thinking they're about to get pounded—and then just gently smooth your hair instead. It's a classic, and the Butcher was the master, like a gunslinger. He had even perfected the two-handed hair-smooth move, making kids on both sides of him fall to pieces simultaneously.

The Butcher caused tears to fall like rain. Apparently, Stephen Jablowski (the poor kid who'd gotten slammed into the locker on my first day) would blubber at the mention of the word "Gerald." (Or "hair," or "smooth," or "move.") Jablowski cried almost constantly. You'd hear his eerie wail off in the distance . . . like a sickly coyote.

But the Butcher would never make me come unglued, and he wouldn't make me cry. Ever. If my mom couldn't do it by dying, how could some blowhard bully do it?

At Mom's funeral, everybody cried but me. I was just mad. Mad at the jerks on the street that I could see through the tinted window of the limo. How could they not know that the whole world had changed? How could they ride bikes and eat ice cream and laugh their stupid laughs? I hated the way people treated me, too. Always making sad faces, like I was so pathetic. For a while I was sick of everyone, even the people who were just trying to be nice.

But creeps like the Butcher were in a whole different category. I was really, really, super sick of his particular brand of nincompoop.

I went back to minding my own scribbling at the cafeteria table. Actually, I was inspired to draw a lovely portrait of the Butcher. And by lovely, I mean lovely flaming insects flying out of his lovely piggish nose. I heard him and his goons snickering about me, but I didn't even react. That was what the Butcher wanted, and I refused to give him the satisfaction. It didn't matter, anyway. My drawings would give me the secret last laugh.

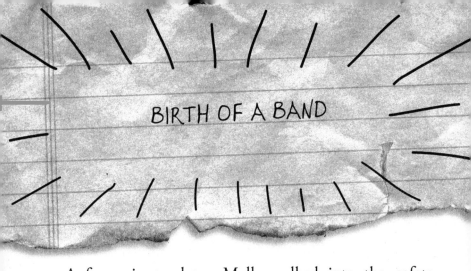

BIRTH OF A BAND

A few minutes later, Molly walked into the cafeteria, picked up a tray, and got in line. She disappeared through a door with all the other suckers eagerly awaiting generous portions of Wilson's finest slop to shovel down their gullets. After approximately forever, she emerged . . . and walked toward *me*. It was one of those slow-motion things. I was trying to hide the fact that I was watching her, but I probably didn't hide it very well.

Molly's hair bounced perfectly as she passed right by and sat down at the table behind me . . . with *Edwin*. They chatted like old friends, catching up on what had happened so far that day. I couldn't hear much, despite the fact that I was eavesdropping with all my might, but

one thing that Molly said stuck out: "It would be cool to start a band, which is why we definitely won't do it."

Okay, so like I said, Mom always told me to look for openings exactly like this to strike up conversations with people, but I hardly ever do. In fact, I never do. But I knew this could be my ticket to talk to Molly, and those kinds of tickets were hard to come by.

I grabbed my tray and notebook and stood up. It was like my body took over. My brain was screaming, "Stop, loser! Go back!" but my legs somehow delivered me to Molly and Edwin's table. I felt a hunk of UFO drip inside my collar, down my back, and onto the floor. I prayed that nobody had noticed that bit of weirdness.

"Excuse me," I mumbled, not looking at them, "did someone say something about starting a band? Because I was in one back at my old school. I play guitar a little. Not that well, but, you know . . . *okay*. So anyway, I'm interested. In starting a band, I mean." It sounded unbelievably lame coming out of my mouth. I was absolutely positive that this was another thing I had screwed up before it even got started.

"Sounds good to me," said Molly simply.

Wait, what?

"Sounds good to her, new kid," said Edwin.

I couldn't believe my ears.

"Okay, well . . . by the way, I'm Davis Delaware," I said, pulling up a chair.

"We already know that," said Edwin. "So, what's Delaware like?"

Here we go again. "I've never even been to Delaware. I'm from Newark, just an hour and a half away."

"Are you sure?" asked Edwin. "There *is* a Newark in Delaware."

"I know," I said. "But I'm from Newark, *New York*."

"You must mean New *Jersey*," said Edwin.

Most people think that Newark, New York—my hometown on the Erie Canal, halfway between Rochester and Syracuse—is a typo. But Edwin was clearly messing with me.

CANADA

LAKE ONTARIO

← BUFFALO (NOT THE HUGE SHAGGY ANIMAL) • GREECE (NY!) [pronounced LIONS not the French way!] The new town →

ERIE CANAL LYONS

ROCHESTER PALMYRA NEWARK (NY, NOT NJ) SYRACUSE
(NOT THE CITY IN ENGLAND OR JACK BENNY'S SIDEKICK) (NOT THE ANCIENT SYRIAN CITY) (NOT THE ANCIENT GREEK CITY)

• GENEVA NOT SWITZERLAND!

FINGER LAKES → • ITHACA (NOT THE HOME OF ODYSSEUS)

"New *York*," I said.

"Wait, I'm confused," he continued, scratching his head. "Why on Earth did you tell us you were from Delaware, then?"

"Were you dropped on your head as a child?" I asked.

That made Edwin smile.

"Really, Edwin," said Molly, raising an eyebrow at him and then turning to me. "Hi, I'm Molly."

Like I didn't know that.

"This is cool," she went on, "because maybe for once something not totally boring might actually happen around here. This pathetic excuse for a school might finally have another band besides the Butchers, who don't even write their own material or anything." She leaned back in her chair. "And amazingly, this miracle has come to us from some new kid named Davis who, despite what he said at first, is not from Delaware. It's also a relief that he can actually talk, and not just squawk like a bird."

So, she did hear that. Good god. But then she smiled in a way that made it funny. It's the kind of teasing you don't mind getting from a girl.

"Yeah," I said, "the Butchers are lame." I'd never heard them play, but it was Gerald's band, so I hated them automatically. I went a little further. "Plus, you're right, any band that doesn't write their own stuff sucks big-time."

"You write songs?" said Molly.

"Me? No, never . . . not really, no," I said. Of course,

I had written lots of songs. Why couldn't I just *tell* her that?

"So, you want our band to suck?" asked Edwin.

Molly made a fake sad face.

I backpedaled. "No, no . . . I guess I could try to write one . . . a song, I mean."

"Great," she said, pushing away from the table. "Then it's settled. I challenge Davis Not From Delaware to write a song, and we'll hear it Friday after school. We just need a place to practice."

"Barbershop," said Edwin.

"Barbershop?" I repeated.

"Is there an echo in here?" Edwin asked.

"I gotta go," said Molly, standing up and looking at me. "Edwin's dad's barbershop is perfect."

She was the one who was perfect. I tilted my head back—way back—to avoid looking like I was ogling her. Which I was. I even covered my mouth, because I was afraid it was hanging wide open.

"See ya," she said, heading for the tray return.

Why couldn't I stop being shy? Just be a different person? It was probably in my DNA. I had the bashful gene. I was predestined for debilitating shyness. Even in this whole new place, where people didn't know every single chapter of my miserable life story, I still couldn't shake the shyness. After all, they had no idea that, back in elementary school, I'd gotten beaten up by a girl.

Sure, Sally Bean was a *large* girl with a thicker mustache in first grade than Gerald had now—but still. Plus, these new people didn't know I had wet my pants at the top of the slide. I'd just won an orange-soda drinking contest against Randy Ross, who was a sore loser and followed me up the ladder and kicked me in the back just as I pushed off, so there was a good reason. Except that there's no good reason. Wetting your pants is still wetting your pants. No point in trying to explain it. The more you try, the worse it gets. Believe me. Anyway, I came down the slide and Sally Bean was standing, facing me at the bottom, ready to attack. I have no idea why. All I know is that the pee got there first. Sally screamed, and I slid right into her fist. She fell on top of me and rolled me over and over in the sand.

Walking into class with a bloody nose and

peed-in pants with sand stuck all over the crotch is something no one ever forgets. Even though Sally moved away the next year, to some kids I would always be "Urine Trouble," "Pee Boy," or the "Slip Slide Kid."

Those wonderful nicknames got carved into my desks and lockers and written on blackboards and walls for years. They were yelled out in gym class  and whispered during exams. Somebody wrote "Urine Trouble, Pee Boy" on the back of my shirt once and I wore it all day. Nice.

In this new school, in a new town, no one knew about any of that. Molly and Edwin only knew that I had been in a band. That was technically true, but it was 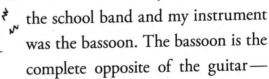 the school band and my instrument was the bassoon. The bassoon is the complete opposite of the guitar—a chick anti-magnet. Girls are instantly repelled into space if they come within

twenty feet of a bassoon-blowing buffoon. From that day forward, when it comes to the bassoonist, those girls permanently reside on Planet Bug Off, Dimwit.

I did play the guitar a little. Just not in a band. And not outside my room. But it turned out that my new bandmates were even worse.

"I had one lesson on the bass," Edwin said, leaning back in his chair, with his feet up on the cafeteria table. "That's all it took. The guy ran out of stuff to teach me."

Yeah, right.

"Molly thinks she's a good singer," he continued. "But during assembly last year, the music teacher told her to stop singing and just mouth the words."

Great. So I was in a bad band. But it was the bad band that Molly was in.

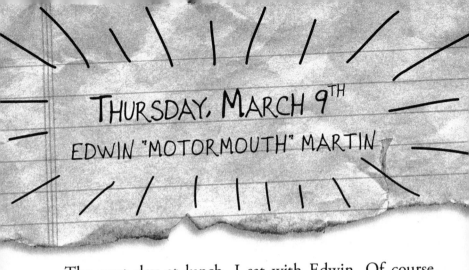

The next day at lunch, I sat with Edwin. Of course, I already knew he loved to talk, but I had never witnessed this kind of word tsunami. He told me that he was the smartest kid in school and Molly was the second smartest, and Gerald hated that. Gerald had tormented him for years. Once, Gerald stuffed grated carrots up Edwin's nose.

"I thought I'd die of root-vegetable inhalation," he said. "I actually went to the nurse's office and then to the emergency room. The doctor had to gas me and use

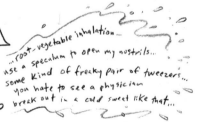

...root-vegetable inhalation...
use a speculum to open my nostrils...
some kind of freaky pair of tweezers...
you hate to see a physician
break out in a cold sweat like that...

a speculum to open my nostrils and retrieve the orange shavings with some kind of freaky pair of tweezers. Afterward, the guy gave a huge sigh of relief. He was shaking from nerves. You hate to see a physician break out in a cold sweat like that. He said that if the carrots had made their way down into my lungs, it would have been bad—so-long-it's-been-good-to-know-you bad."

Did I mention that Edwin liked to talk?

"I've known Molly since we were little. Our moms were friends," he explained. Unprompted. "My dad is a barber and his shop is connected to our house, which is no reason to make fun of someone, but everyone does. When I get out of Harvard Business School, I'm gonna build my parents a mansion with a solid-gold barbershop and a fifty-foot barber pole and a full-time barber to cut my dad's hair. He'll trim it at the exact rate it's growing so it'll never look like a new haircut, always perfect."

"Good plan," I said, thinking he was finally finished. Nothing doing.

"Plus, a spa for my mom. She'll get massaged with fancy soaps while watching soaps on TV all day. Gerald will be her personal slave and toilet licker. When he screws up, I'll stick carrots or kitty litter or anything else that happens to be lying around up his nose, or an orifice of my choosing to be named later."

I didn't think Edwin would ever stop, but then he did. Suddenly. I could see from his face that someone had walked up behind me.

I had a feeling I knew who it was.

GERALD, UP CLOSE AND PERSONAL

"Get a load of the dweeb twins," the Butcher announced. "Old Dweeb and New Dweeb." The creeps who constantly huddled around him snickered and wheezed like a bunch of giant cartoon rodents.

He obviously meant "dweeb" as a big insult, but after he said it, I blurted out: "Wow, how did you know that the Dweebs happens to be the name of our band?"

The Butcher and Edwin looked at me like I had lost my mind. Maybe I had.

"It's the *Amazing* Dweebs, actually," I continued. "But I guess you already knew that from reading that magazine article about us." I sometimes lie when I'm threatened.

"Oh, right," Gerald said. "Was that *Dumb Dweeb Times* or *Moronic Dweeb Weekly*?"

"Oh, it was a magazine you have to be slightly cool to know about," I said. I was obviously getting into dangerous territory. That remark could have landed me in traction. But it was the least of my problems.

Because Edwin was apparently encouraged by my wisecrack.

The last-word freak broke his silence with this helpful tidbit: "Davis here mentioned something interesting earlier. He said that the Butchers suck. Actually, I believe his exact words were that the Butchers 'suck big-time.'"

What a blabbermouth.

The Butcher growled like a pit bull.

But one of his goons made a different sound: *"Ewwwwwwww!"*

I thought it was a weird reaction until I realized that he was *ewwing* about something else entirely. Assistant Goon had grabbed my notebook.

"Hey," he said, nudging Gerald, "check out New Dweeb's gross cartoon of you."

Gerald

Assistant Goon ripped out the page and threw the notebook on the floor. The Butcher snatched the cartoon, eyeballed it, and tore it to shreds. Thank goodness they didn't notice the song on the next page: *way* more insulting. The drawing was bad enough.

The Butcher's face turned purple.

"Now you did it, dweeb," he hissed, looking around, checking for witnesses. The cafeteria ladies weren't far away. I guess that's why he decided against just plain murdering me. "Don't move, and don't make a sound," he whispered, grabbing my earlobe. He squeezed hard. And twisted.

"Ahh!" I gasped.

"C'mon, Butcher," said Edwin.

"Not a sound, dweebs," he repeated.

I'm pretty sure he would have ripped my entire ear off, but just then Principal Rigo walked into the cafeteria. He was giving a tour to some happy parents and unhappy future students.

"Oh, look," said Gerald, loudly and insincerely, "there's a little piece of food on your ear there. Let me get that for you." He let go and pretended to flick something with his finger and thumb. My ear was throbbing.

"As you can see," said the principal, smiling at the tour group, "we encourage our students to help each other out

whenever they can. It's an important part of the Wilson philosophy. Makes you proud. Carry on, boys."

The kids on the tour rolled their eyes. They knew an alpha goon when they saw one. They could imagine coming to this school and having *their* ears abused. They probably pictured all kinds of horrors. But the parents nodded their heads, like Rigo was some sort of educational genius or something. "I'd love to hear more about that philosophy," gushed one excited mom as she followed Rigo into the hallway.

Once they'd left, Gerald leaned in close. I could smell his sweat and his UFO breath. "The good news is, you won't be New Dweeb for long," he hissed. "Soon you'll be *Dead* Dweeb."

He walked away. By then, the throbbing had spread

from my ear to my brain. I picked up my notebook and tried to act like what had happened didn't bother me at all.

"What a moron," I grumbled to Edwin.

I was glad Molly wasn't there to witness that — until I realized she was standing in the doorway. I wasn't sure if she'd just gotten there or if she'd watched the whole thing. Fantastic.

Gerald and his entire pack of goons were moving in her direction. They all passed by Molly, except Gerald. He stopped and stared at her. Up close. What, was he going to harass her, too? He was saying something I couldn't hear, and he put his huge hand on her shoulder.

I had to do something. I mean, the guy was a psychopath. I started to get up — and that's when it happened.

Gerald slid his hand around the back of Molly's neck, pulled her in . . . and kissed her.

Serious lip-lock. She pushed him away, but not like she hated him. Not like, *Get your filthy foul mouth away from me, you disgusting orangutan.* More like, *Not now, you mildly irritating boyfriend who has kissed me many times before.*

After seeing that, I kind of wished Gerald had just killed me. Or at least poked my eyes out.

"Behold the first couple of Woodrow Wilson," said Edwin flatly.

What? I was too horrified to speak. How was this possible? Molly was so great, and Gerald was so *not* great, such a Neanderthal. What was there to like about that idiot?

Good god, he was putting his arm around her. But as they turned to walk away, she brushed the arm away and snapped at him, loudly enough for me to hear.

"Don't you dare lay a finger on my bandmate ever again, *Gerald*." She said "Gerald" like it was a dirty word.

So that made it better, but only a little. I never really thought Molly would go for me, anyway. I mean, I let myself fantasize about it, but deep down I knew it would never happen. After witnessing this revolting display, even the fantasy part had to stop. Molly was a great girl and everything, but now I doubted her sanity.

Plus, I wasn't going to fight the Butcher over her in a gazillion years. I enjoyed breathing too much.

For the rest of the day, I couldn't stop thinking about how weird it was that Molly was with the Butcher. How does something like that even come about? Just contemplating it made me kind of depressed. I mean, if girls were only

looking for muscles and money,
I didn't stand a chance.

Molly's song challenge worked on me, though. I wrote three or four songs in my note book that after-noon. I didn't pay much attention to school. In fact, I really can't remember much of anything that happened, or anything I learned. I was too busy thinking about the next day: our first practice as the Amazing Dweebs.

FRIDAY, MARCH 10TH
BARBERSHOP TRIO

Edwin, Molly, and I met at the barbershop that Friday night. It was sort of weird. For one thing, the whole place reeked of hair product. And those combs in blue liquid creeped me out, like some kind of freaky aliens floating in formaldehyde. But with the mirrors and barber chair, it felt like a set for a music video or something. We spun each other around in the chair with our feet up until we all felt sick. Sick in a good way.

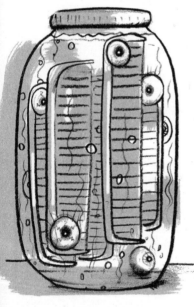

Edwin's mom brought in a tray of milk and cookies and put it on the marble counter, right next to the alien specimens. The ceiling lamp shone through the blue liquid, giving the milk an unappetizing glow.

"Rock stars need energy," she said in the sweetest,

nicest voice ever. It was hard to believe she was related to Edwin.

"Mom," said Edwin, "rock stars don't eat milk and cookies. Whiskey and huge quantities of prescription medication is more like it."

"Yeah," I added, "and afterward we'll bust up the barbershop like a hotel room." I thought Edwin's mom would laugh, but she didn't. Edwin gave me a totally fake shocked look, even though his joke had been way more shocking.

"So you must be Davis," Mrs. Martin said, shaking her head while shaking my hand.

"Yes . . . that was a joke, by the way."

"I realize, dear." Weird, but it didn't bother me when *she* called me "dear." She sort of reminded me of a grandmother, and grandmothers can call you whatever they want.

"Not all jokes can be funny," said Edwin.

"You would know," I replied.

"So I hear you moved here from Delaware," said Mrs. Martin.

"That's right," said Edwin, "the whiskey capital of the world. Toddlers pour it on their cornflakes there."

"Okay, then," his mom said, rolling her eyes and heading back into the house.

"Thanks for the cookies, Mrs. Martin," said Molly.

"Even though we're not eating them," chirped Edwin with obviously fake cheerfulness. He waited until the door slammed and then quickly scarfed a fistful of cookies, almost without chewing.

The kid was a mystery to me.

"So," said Molly, suddenly staring me down like a cop looking for answers, "where's the big song?"

"I've got it," I said, "but don't you feel like twirling in the chair some more?"

"C'mon, Delaware, while we're still young," said Edwin, inhaling another small mountain of cookies. He didn't even stop talking to eat. "Unless you didn't write one. No big deal if you didn't. I mean, we won't like you any less. Well, maybe a little less. But we won't HATE you. Maybe just a tiny dose of hate. Certainly not a super-sized serving of hate."

"Edwin, do you get paid by the *word*?" I asked, looking to see if Molly would smile. She did.

"Not yet," said Edwin.

I opened my guitar case, grabbed my notebook, and ripped the song out. Then I closed the notebook immediately, not wanting them to see anything else in there.

I handed the page to Molly and she read the title: "The Amazing Dweebs Theme Song?"

"Oh, right," I said, checking her face for signs of disgust, wondering if I'd just blown the whole deal. "You weren't around when we came up with the band's name."

"What do you mean, *we*?" snapped Edwin.

Molly shook her head. She wasn't a dweeb in real life, like I probably was. And like Edwin definitely was. No, she was just the opposite. But that made the possibility of her singing the song even cooler. It takes nerve to tell the world you're a dweeb, especially if you're not. I was pretty sure Molly had the guts to pull it off.

She read the lyrics to herself and then looked at me again. "Not exactly a Grammy winner."

"Good songs don't win Grammys," I said. "The Beatles never won a Grammy. Neither did Jimi Hendrix." I plugged my guitar into Edwin's amp, which popped and echoed a bit.

"Yeah, whatever," said Edwin. "I totally thought you were kidding about that Amazing Dweeb thing."

It was hard to defend, but I tried: "Well, it's so un-cool, it's *cool* . . . you know?"

They furrowed their brows and looked at me like I had more than one screw loose. Like they weren't so sure about what they'd gotten themselves into. I wasn't so sure, either.

Luckily, that uncomfortable moment was interrupted by a loud knock on the barbershop door. The force of the pounding swung the door open.

Unluckily, there stood the Butcher.

He was wearing one of those super-gross sleeveless 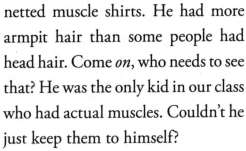 netted muscle shirts. He had more armpit hair than some people had head hair. Come *on*, who needs to see that? He was the only kid in our class who had actual muscles. Couldn't he just keep them to himself?

He shook his head at Molly. "I heard that you came over here. What kind of stupid band practices in a barbershop?"

I was trying to think of a snappy comeback, but Molly came back first: "Shut your piehole, *Gerald.*"

What a girl.

"We gotta talk, Moll," growled the Butcher.

"Start talking, *Gerald*."

"Not here."

"Well, this is where I am. *GERALD*."

"Stop *calling* me that—"

"What, you mean your name?" she said.

I decided this was a good time to start the song. I strummed lightly on my guitar.

I sang softly at first, but Gerald kept talking, so I got louder and louder.

We're not that popular
Around the school . . .

Edwin started slamming away at the bass. Molly smiled and looked back down at the song's lyrics. Gerald steamed.

The Amazing Dweebs!
The Amazing Dweebs!

Molly held the paper up between us. Soon, all three Dweebs were hamming it up, loudly.

Uh-huh, that's right . . .
The Amazing Dweebs!

The Butcher covered his ears. "I don't understand

why all of a sudden you want to be a dweeb and hang around with dweebs and be in a dweeb band!" he yelled, storming out the door. "This is the worst dweeb crap ever!"

I had to agree, it did sound horrible. But quality had nothing to do with it. It was dumb—the right kind of dumb.

You say we're nerds,
You say we're nuts,
Just watch us while
We kick your butts!
The Amazing Dweebs!
The Amazing Dweebs!
Uh-huh, that's right . . .
The Amazing Dweebs!

Edwin and I played so hard we both broke strings. My finger got bloody and my fingernail snapped. (I never use a guitar pick. I always lose them, so I just keep the nail on my index finger kind of long.) Molly danced around the barbershop, using a hairbrush for a microphone. Watching a girl like Molly dance really makes you realize

why dancing was invented. She sort of went back and forth between dancing well and dancing dorky, but it all worked for her.

We sang the simple chorus over and over, screaming, then whispering, then screaming again. We didn't stop until our voices were shot.

Talk about amazing. I couldn't believe I was letting other people see this part of me. They actually joined in on something I wrote. Plus, it was cool that we were able to get so crazy together. There's nothing better than acting like a lunatic with other people who are also acting like lunatics.

We twirled each other around in the barber chair some more. When we twirled Molly, she was smiling with her eyes closed. Her cheeks got red, and every time she came around she was more beautiful. But I was trying not to think about that.

SATURDAY, MARCH 11TH & SUNDAY, MARCH 12TH
ONE SONG LEADS TO ANOTHER

That weekend, I couldn't stop. I wrote songs about what jerks Gerald and his goons were, about how boring school was, about bad teachers and clueless adults. I had a guitar on my lap and a pencil in my hand for two whole days. I had the amp turned up loud. I went through three notebooks.

Dad knocked on the door at about seven thirty Sunday night. He had to pound pretty hard because of the racket I was making.

"Davis, I'm home! You hungry?"

We had the classic Dad dinner: spaghetti, peas, bread. I never realized how good my mom's food was until Dad started cooking. Spaghetti's okay, but the sauce he makes is super-watery and it seeps into the other stuff on the plate. The bread turns pink and mushy and the pea juice gets in there, too, and it's ultra-disgusting. I love bread. It's very hard to make bread taste bad.

My dad makes bread taste bad.

The cure for his cooking is shaky cheese, lots and lots of shaky cheese. There wasn't much left in the container that night, so I shook it hard. The only sound in the room was the rattling of Parmesan pebbles.

Rattle, rattle.

"So, all in all, how was your first week?"

Rattle, rattle, rattle.

"Five days of nonstop misery."

Rattle, rattle, rattle, rattle.

I knew my dad wasn't feeling so great about the move or his job, and he probably missed Mom even more than I did. For a long time, I thought about her pretty much every minute. The sadness was like a bully that got right up in your face.

Every single square inch of our old house reminded me of her. I could barely look into the living room. The piano was the worst. You could see the dust on the bench from the doorway. When I was little, I would sit next to her while she played. She didn't even mind when I banged on the keys, really screwing up the piece she

was practicing. Sometimes we would
"play a rainstorm" together. We'd start
by lightly hammering tiny raindrops on
the high notes, then make the rain come
down louder and lower and faster, then
jab lightning strikes on the middle notes,
and finally pound out thunder with our fists and elbows.
I'd step on the pedal for a loud, echoing rumble. Then
we'd slow it down, and work our way back up to the high
plinky notes until the rain stopped. With the last few
drops we'd collapse onto the keys and each other.

I avoided my dad's room, too. When I walked by the
door, I imagined her in there, and I didn't want to see
that she wasn't.

Dad and I tried really hard to cheer each other up
after she died, but soon we knew it wasn't working. It
couldn't work. Our cheerfulness was ridiculously fake.
We were like bad actors who couldn't convince anybody,
especially ourselves.

We got tired of trying.

Now, a year and a half later, we had moved into a new
house, which was good. But we'd settled into a different
kind of sadness. More like dullness. My mom and dad
used to goof around and sometimes even sing together
while she cooked or they cleaned up after dinner. My
dad would sing "The Man on the Flying Trapeze."

I especially liked that one when I was little because it was also in an old Popeye cartoon:

He floats through the air with the greatest of ease,
The daring young man on the flying trapeze,
His movements are graceful, all girls he does please,
But my love he has stolen away.

Dad really hammed it up as they waltzed around the room. I couldn't imagine my dad singing now. He hardly even smiled. Then again, neither did I. Numb was the new normal in the Delaware house. Of course, I sang in my room, but it wasn't that super-happy-dancing-around-the-kitchen kind. It was more like the everything-has-gone-to-hell-and-that's-why-I-hate-the-world kind.

Meanwhile, a whole new something was happening outside of the house. I liked hanging around with Molly and Edwin, and I loved the idea of writing songs for the Dweebs. I felt kind of guilty that things were going better for me all of a sudden. I was afraid it would make my dad feel even worse, so I just didn't tell him.

"I've got a ton of homework," I said, excusing myself from the table.

But I didn't do homework. I went back to my guitar and notebook. I just turned the volume down this time.

SONG #2:
GET OUTTA MY FACE
By Davis Delaware

Get outta my face! Get outta my face!
Get outta my town! Get outta this place!
You just hanging 'round is bringing down the
  human race,
Get outta my face! Get outta my face!

Get outta my sight! Get outta my sight!
You're such a pain! All day and night!
So many words describe you, but they
  wouldn't be polite,
Get outta my sight! Get outta my sight!

Get outta my face! Get outta my face!
Get outta my school! Get outta this place!
Maybe you should blast off and get lost in
  outer space,
Get outta my face! Get outta my face!

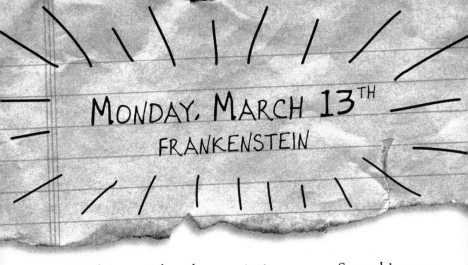

MONDAY, MARCH 13TH
FRANKENSTEIN

I woke up with a sharp pain in my eye. Something was stuck to my eyebrow. I peeled it off. *Owww!* I had fallen asleep on my notebook's spiral binding. I glanced over at the alarm clock that I had forgotten to set.

I was incredibly late.

I leaped up and looked in the mirror. The spiral had made dents in my flesh from forehead to cheek. It looked a lot like stitches. Luckily, I'd fallen asleep in my clothes and I live close to school. No time for breakfast or a shower. I just bolted out the door.

I could still feel the "stitches" on my face when I ran into Miss Danderbrook's first-period English class six minutes later, just as the bell rang. Made it.

We were all taking our seats when Danderbrook stood up in front of her desk and addressed us.

"Okay, class," she singsonged, like a preschool teacher. "Pass your poems forward!"

Poems? I was instantly nauseous. I forgot to write a stinking poem. I must have groaned out loud.

"Davis," she said, "is there a problem? And *ouch*, what happened to your face? Were you in an accident over the weekend?"

"No . . . no . . ." I said, rifling through my stuff. I acted confused, whispering loudly. "Now where the heck did I put that poem? I worked so hard on it . . ." I pretended to be outraged. "Okay, who's been messing with my stuff?"

Edwin snickered, shook his head, and passed his poem to the front.

Molly smiled over at me and raised an eyebrow. "Nice scar, Frankenstein." She handed in her poem, too.

Everyone had poems but me.

I kept shuffling papers, not wanting to make eye contact with Danderbrook. But she wasn't falling for it. She'd been teaching for a long time, and she'd seen everything. I flipped through my notebook, trying not to panic.

That's when I realized that the songs I'd been writing looked a heck of a lot like poetry.

I didn't even think about which one to grab. As long as it was it was shaped like a poem, it would work.

"Got it!" I cried, ripping a page out . . . and almost in half. Ugh. I went to tear out another "poem." Any one would do.

But then I heard a *"Pssst!"* Molly was holding out one of those little plastic Scotch tape rolls. "Catch!" she whispered, tossing it over. I reached for it, but instead tipped it into the air — then again and again, from fingertip to fingertip — like an insane person playing volleyball with himself. It got a laugh, but I did finally catch the thing.

"Thanks," I said to Molly, quickly taping the poem back together. I got up and slipped the crudely mended sheet into the middle of the stack of perfectly typed pages at the front of the room.

Danderbrook looked at me like I was totally nuts. "Is that it, or do you have an encore?" she asked.

Another laugh.

"No, sorry, that's it," I said, feeling relieved that at least I had something to turn in. But Danderbrook wasn't finished.

"Wonderful," she replied, pulling the sheet back out of the stack with her thumb and forefinger. She made a face and held it up like it might infect her. "I simply cannot wait to grade that. Is this what was expected of students in Delaware?"

"No," I said, not even bothering to correct her.

"Always nice to get off to a fresh start in a new school," she said.

DINNER CONVERSATION

At dinner that night (leftover Chinese, dried out, possibly moldy), I was still thinking about Molly. *Nice scar, Frankenstein.*

"Anything happen in school today?" Dad asked.

"Nope."

"Nothing?"

"Nothing."

"Nothing *at all*?"

"Nothing. At. All. Big fat zip-zilch-nada of a day."

"Meet anybody new?"

"Negative."

He stopped eating and looked at me. "How could you not meet anyone new? Everyone *there* is new to you."

"Yeah, well, I didn't meet any of them." I decided to change the subject. "Did you meet anyone new at work?"

"We weren't talking about me."

"Well, I wasn't talking about *me*."

"Okay, okay," he said. He paused for a minute.

"Listen, Davis, remember how we used to go camping and fishing when you were younger?"

"Yeah . . ." I knew where this was going and I didn't want to go.

"Well, you have a long weekend coming up, and I was wondering if you'd like to take a little trip up to the woods with me. You could bring a friend along if you want." Dad was obviously trying.

"I don't know, maybe," I said. "It sounds great, but I've got tons of homework."

"Okay, well, you think about it," he said, getting up from the table. He put his plate in the sink, then went on. "Oh, and by the way, I signed you up for karate. It'll be a good way to get to know other kids."

"WHAT?"

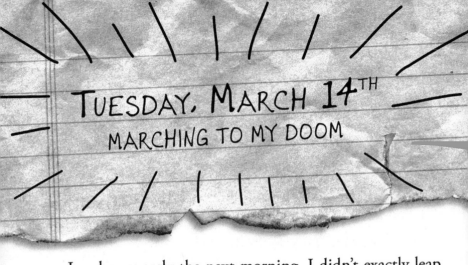

TUESDAY, MARCH 14TH
MARCHING TO MY DOOM

I woke up early the next morning. I didn't exactly leap out of bed, though. Instead, I listened to the rain for a while.

Dad tapped on the door. "Are you awake in there? Better get up. Gotta go, bye!"

"Bye."

The rain stopped by the time I left the house, but when I was a block from school, a truck blew by, plowing through a deep puddle. About a hundred gallons of water landed on me. Instant wet rat.

As I entered the building, the squish-squashing of my sneakers echoed in the hallway. I passed Molly. She was quietly arguing with the Butcher. I prayed that neither one of them would notice me. Edwin slammed his locker and walked alongside me.

"Take a shower with your clothes on?" he asked.

"Funny. Stop talking," I grumbled. I wasn't in the mood.

But, of course, he didn't. Edwin was incapable of that. "Dear me!" He imitated me in a voice like a squeaky Muppet. "Where the heck is my poem? Who's been messing with my stuff? I worked so *hard* on it!"

Ha, ha.

When we got into the classroom, Danderbrook was clutching the stack of poems in her arms. I sloshed to my seat. A large puddle formed on the floor under my chair.

"Do you have your own personal rain cloud, Frankenstein?" Molly asked, slipping into her chair.

"Okay, people," said Danderbrook, now sounding like a *severely depressed* preschool teacher. "This should not have been a tough assignment. All it required was a teeny bit of effort. You couldn't harm a fly with the effort expended on most of these poems. A *fruit* fly. A *baby* fruit fly. That's why tonight's

homework assignment is the same as your last homework assignment. That's right . . . start over."

"Awwwwwwwwww," every- one groaned. Everyone but me. I was just glad I wasn't the only one who had screwed up.

"However," she said, "there is one student I think we should hear from."

Everyone looked at Edwin, who smiled.

"I'd like that student to come up and read to the class," Danderbrook continued.

Edwin stood up.

"No, Edwin, not you. It can't *always* be you."

This made Molly smile, and she got up. After all, she was the only other obvious contender.

"Davis Delaware," Danderbrook said, waving Molly away and giving me a heart attack, "please do us the honor of reading your work."

What?

I glanced over at Molly and Edwin, who looked at each other in disbelief and slowly sat back down. Danderbrook held out my mangled poem.

She was doing this to embarrass me. I knew it. It seemed kind of mean, especially since I was a new kid and everything. Why me? What did I do to deserve this?

I sloshed toward the front of the room, preparing for a megadose of humiliation. She handed me the paper. I held it up in front of my face and looked at the title: "Watch the Melting Clock." What was I thinking? This song was about Danderbrook, and she had obviously figured it out. It was about me being bored out of my mind in her class a few days earlier.

I'd been staring at the clock, praying the minute hand would budge during my lifetime. The second hand seemed to be ticking backward. It was incredibly hot, and a trickle of sweat had dripped off my nose and onto the page. It had landed on the face of a drawing I'd done of myself, causing the ink to run like a watercolor.

That's when I had thought of Salvador Dalí. I've always liked that painting with the melting pocket watches. It's called *The Persistence of Memory*, but I just call it the melty-clock painting. I never really even knew what the heck it was supposed to mean, but at that moment I'd felt like I was *living* in it. I'd imagined the clock dripping down the classroom wall. I'd looked back

at my notebook, and my head had spread into a big blue blob. Danderbrook was melting my brain and ticking my life away.

So, here we were. My poem had insulted old lady Danderbrook, and now she wanted payback in front of the whole class. I was brand-new at this school and already screwed. This poem would be my new "Urine Trouble, Pee Boy."

"Please, Mr. Delaware," she said, gesturing for me to start reading.

I hid behind the wrinkled, taped-up page and mumbled, "Watch the Melting Clock."

"Speak up," said Danderbrook.

The paper rattled in my sweaty fingers. Someone snickered.

Danderbrook snapped. "ZIP IT! You would all do well to listen up. This poem's presentation — its wrinkled, distressed appearance, the tear, the tape — has been carefully designed to express its theme: the ravages of time. Mr. Delaware has written a breathtaking and mature examination of the nature of mortality. He even went to the trouble of faking scars on his face yesterday and hosing himself down today to reinforce that theme. The fact that he chose to write it as a Shakespearean sonnet — getting a bit playful with the structure, using eight instead of ten syllables per line—only makes his poem's somber reflection that much more resonant within the context of classical literature."

Excuse me?

What the heck was she talking about? She had to be kidding, except I could tell from the look on her face that she wasn't. I had written a sonnet . . . well, *almost* a sonnet . . . *accidentally*? Was that even possible? I'd had to write one back at my old school earlier in the year, and I guess I just fell into the basic format.

I glanced over at Molly. She looked beautiful even with her mouth hanging open. On the other hand, Edwin's eyes seemed like they might pop out, bounce off his desk, and roll out the door. The class looked like a roomful of spooked raccoons.

I had entered the twilight zone. A *good* twilight zone.

"Please continue, Davis," Danderbrook said, squinting and biting her lip. She seemed to be drifting into some sort of poetry trance. Miss Dolores Danderbrook, twenty-year veteran of the public school system, was trembling like a leaf. She was under my spell.

SONG #3
WATCH THE MELTING CLOCK
By Davis Delaware

The kids all watch the melting clock,
Drip down the wall like wax in flame,
Like lambs they're slaughtered with the flock,
The sleep is deep and who's to blame?

The heat, the blood, the sweat, the tears,
Like lava burning hours and days,
The boring months, the wasted years,
Beneath the geezer's ancient gaze.

The children all will someday lie,
In sands of time turned into mud,
Surrender now, for soon you die,
Forgotten in a pool of blood.

You kick and scream and push and shove,
You'll never kiss the one you love.

I almost choked up at the end, and realized I was thinking less about Danderbrook and Molly at that point, and more about Mom.

Miss Danderbrook was *weeping*. Did she know about my mother? Probably. Everyone probably knew. That kind of thing gets around. Danderbrook's mouth had turned into such an intensely sad frown it seemed like she was exaggerating like a French mime, but she wasn't. It was real.

Molly was sniffling, too. Cissy Seabrook cried so hard she started choking. Another girl walked around passing out Kleenex, like a funeral director or something. Noses were honking like car horns in traffic. Edwin and the other guys weren't actually shedding tears, but they were definitely stunned. I had meant for the song to be funny and maybe angry, but I guess it was a whole lot sadder as a poem.

Turned out, Danderbrook *loved* sad. She said she would feature my poem in the next poetry club magazine, even though I wasn't in poetry club. Until about five seconds earlier, I hadn't even liked poetry.

I could only think that Danderbrook was so excited that someone put a tiny bit of work into the assignment that she sort of overreacted. If I had just spoken those kinds of things, she would have called me a whiny brat who didn't appreciate all that life and English class had to offer. But throw in a little rhyme and rhythm and she got all blubbery. Of course, she didn't notice that the poem was about *her*, that *she* was the "geezer." I have to admit, the whole thing made me like her a little more. It's hard not to appreciate someone who appreciates you.

When class was over, Molly touched my shoulder as she passed by, and whispered, "Wow." I tried not to let it make my day, but it did.

Later that afternoon, the Butcher passed me in the hallway between classes and gave me the evil eye . . . with a larger-than-usual dose of evil. He must have gotten word of what went down in English. He pretended to accidentally bump into me, but it felt a lot more like getting hit by a truck. My books went flying. It should have been embarrassing to scramble around

on my hands and knees and gather them up during serious rush-hour foot traffic, but weirdly, it didn't bother me at all.

"Watch the Melting Clock" had changed everything. All of a sudden I was on a roll in English — and my status had gone way up at Woodrow Wilson High.

WEDNESDAY, MARCH 15ᵀᴴ
FURRY

Super news on the home front: leftover spaghetti for dinner. Whoopee. Now it was molded into the shape of the plastic storage container it had spent the past few days entombed in. Dad chopped it in half before he nuked it, and both portions were oddly brick-like. Square-ish pink brains. I couldn't look at the dollops of sauce on top without thinking of blood. The outer noodles were hard, so I scraped out the soft inner noodles, like I was cleaning a fish.

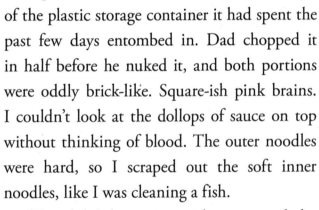

"You didn't happen to pick up some shaky cheese, did you?" I asked. Parmesan is even more essential with secondhand spaghetti.

"No, I got out of work late," said Dad apologetically. "I'll get it tomorrow." He sounded very tired. "Anything new at school?"

"Nope," I lied. I didn't want to make him feel even worse about his day.

"Wow, you'd think in a school of that size, something would eventually happen."

"Yeah, you'd think," I said, getting up and feeding ninety percent of my dinner to the disposal monster. "Hey, Dad, I'm going over to a kid's house to ask him about my homework."

"What kid? Is he a friend?"

I shrugged. "Nah, just some kid who knows what the homework is."

I grabbed my guitar and headed over to the barbershop. Edwin's dad was working late, just finishing up his last haircut of the day: an old dude with nowhere near enough hair to even need to get it cut.

dwin's
dad
↓

"Come on in," Edwin's dad said. "You must be Eddie's friend."

I blinked. "Eddie? Oh, right, Eddie." Only Edwin would prefer being called *Edwin*. "Yes, sir. We started a band."

"Believe me, I know," he said, raising an eyebrow. "The whole neighborhood knows."

I smiled nervously and nodded. If we got kicked out of the barbershop and had to practice unplugged in one of our crummy rooms or something, the band would fall apart. Fast.

Furry

"Oh, c'mon, Walter," said the old dude. "Let 'em use the dang shop. I wanted to play the saxophone as a kid, but after one night of squeaking, my old man returned the thing and told me to forget about music right then and there."

"Probably good advice, Furry," said Mr. Martin.

Furry? Was that his first or last name? Either way, a funny name for a bald dude.

"Good advice if you don't mind wasting your dang life bein' *miserable*!" Furry spat. "I'm eighty-one years old, and I've thought about that saxophone every single day since. I held it in my hands for only ten minutes, seventy years ago. It's too late for me, but for god's sake, let the kids use the dang shop."

"Calm down, Furry," said Edwin's dad. "I heard you the first time."

"Calm down?" Furry was definitely not calm. "Do you know I never walk down Union Street? I go way out of my way. There's a sax in the window of the pawnshop there that just sits and waits for me to pass by so it can laugh at me."

"*Who* laughs at you?" said Edwin, walking through the door.

"A saxophone," I said.

"Never mind," Mr. Martin said. "You guys can play in here. Just turn down the volume."

"*Turn down the volume* is not in the lexicon of rock," said Edwin.

"Neither is *barbershop*, if you don't watch it," said his dad.

"No problem," I put in quickly. "We can turn it down."

Furry looked from Edwin to me and back again. "I'd like to hear you boys play sometime."

"No you wouldn't," said Edwin, shaking his head.

Edwin was right. There was no way an old dude—even a cool old dude—would like the Dweebs. I mean, it would be tough to take for kids who actually *liked* the kind of three-chord-classic-homemade-thrashing-garage-band racket we were trying and failing to achieve.

Molly walked in as Edwin's father and Furry walked out. She was wearing the same Mad Manny the Monkey shirt she wore the first time I saw her. It looked just as good.

"Dang," said Furry, checking her out. "This band is suddenly lookin' a whole lot better."

Okay, that was gross. Furry went from hero to dirty old man in, like, two seconds.

But Molly didn't care. She kissed him on the cheek and said, "Get your weekly cut, Furry?"

"Dang right."

"Good," she said. "I can't have my boyfriend looking all shaggy."

"Okay," Edwin announced, "non–band members out. We gotta practice."

Edwin's dad reminded us to turn down the volume one more time and left to drive Furry home.

"Furry's wife died earlier this year," said Molly once they'd gone.

"RIP, Lady McFurry," said Edwin.

I thought about my mom. There was an uncomfortable pause, and I wondered if Molly and Edwin were thinking about my mom, too. They probably were.

"So," said Molly suddenly, slamming her books down on the counter, "quite an honor to be in the presence of genius."

"Thanks," said Edwin, slowly rotating in the barber chair. "I'm *always* in the presence of genius, even when I'm alone."

"I refer, of course, to our young poetry prodigy,"

Molly clarified, giving Edwin a hard twirl in the chair and giving me a look.

"Ahh, the *new* genius in town," said Edwin, coming around again.

"Okay, okay," I cut in, "are we practicing or what?"

"Does geniuses even *needs* to practice?" asked Molly in a dumber-than-dumb-guy voice.

"Well," I said, noticing a hose and nozzle hooked up to the sink's faucet, "you know what Edison said about genius, right? 'It's one percent inspiration and ninety-nine percent water.'"

"It wasn't *water*," Edwin scoffed, slowly spinning to a stop. "It was *perspiration*."

"No . . ." I said, turning the spigot, the hose bulging from the pressure. "I'm pretty sure it was water."

I spun around and pointed the nozzle at Edwin, my finger ready on the trigger.

"Hey!" he cried, hopping to his feet.

Then I pointed it at Molly.

"You wouldn't."

Then Edwin.

"Whoa, whoa, whoa!"

I turned back toward Molly.

"I dare you." She laughed, holding her hands in front of her face.

Never say dare. I let 'er rip, blasting Molly right in the Mad Manny the Monkey. She screamed from the surprise and the cold, and we all laughed . . . until I realized her T-shirt had become pretty much see-through. I let go of the trigger.

Molly grabbed a bottle of shampoo instead and splooshed me in the eyes.

"AHHHHHHH!" It was like I'd been stung by a bee on my eyeball. I turned the nozzle on my face, but it felt less like rinsing and more like . . . more bees.

And then I heard it. A high-pitched shriek and a *crack*.

I turned around. My eyes were still stinging and swimming in soapy water, so I couldn't see much, but I could tell that Molly was down. She had slipped and smacked her head on the marble floor.

"Molly!" I screamed.

"That's what you get for messing around!" Edwin cried, running for his mom.

I dropped to my knees and lifted Molly's head in my hands. "Wake up!" She was limp. Was she breathing? She looked so beautiful with beads of water on her lashes.

BAM! She socked me in the stomach.

I rolled over, gasping for air. "What was *that*?"

"You gotta admit, it was pretty funny,"

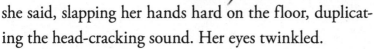

she said, slapping her hands hard on the floor, duplicating the head-cracking sound. Her eyes twinkled.

"I will *not* admit that," said Edwin's mom, running in ahead of Edwin. She looked panicked. And mad.

"Sorry." Molly smiled. "It wasn't funny."

"I agree," said Edwin, smiling now. "Not funny. Not in the slightest. In fact, completely *un-comical*. Utterly devoid of humor. A guaranteed one hundred percent laugh-free zone is what you've got right here."

Molly and I looked at each other. We were trying hard not to laugh. Edwin going on and on about how unfunny it was made it funny.

He held up a finger, like he was about to make a pronouncement. And he did, but in the voice of an incredibly nerdy professor: "Unquestionably, undeniably, *indubitably* un-amusing."

That was it. We all broke down laughing.

Except Edwin's mom.

"Okay, Molly," she said, shaking her head and walking away. "No more hilarious jokes about cracking your skull on the floor, all right? And clean up this mess. Now."

"Here," I said to Molly, "borrow my sweatshirt. I have a T-shirt underneath." I handed her the sweatshirt, and she left with Mrs. Martin to change inside the house.

Within minutes, Molly came back looking great. It means something when a girl and a guy start swapping shirts. In this case it didn't mean very much, and it had better not, because I didn't want anybody getting the wrong idea. Especially not the Butcher. Nobody would even recognize that plain gray sweatshirt as mine, anyway.

But it was cool.

We quickly cleaned up the shop, and I finally got around to figuring out some simple chords for "Watch the Melting Clock." We tried it out, and even though it sounded pretty lousy, I was happy to hear it as a loud, crazy rock song instead of a tortured poem.

"Hey!" said Molly. "I almost forgot. We've been invited to play Rock Around the Dock this year."

"Some invitation," Edwin groaned. "Such a terrible name. I *hate* that thing."

I had no idea what they were even talking about. "What is it?"

"An annual rock concert to kick off spring break," Molly explained. "A benefit for the library. It's a school thing, so the teachers run it with the student council." She wiggled her eyebrows at me. "Your girlfriend Danderbrook is emceeing this year. It happens down at the canal."

"The disgustingly polluted canal," said Edwin. I felt a speech coming on. "If you swim in that crap, it'll kill you. Your brain gets moldy, your private parts fall off, and you slowly bleed to death. If you *swallow* any of it, you die instantly. Word to the wise: If you happen to fall in, just drink up like there's no tomorrow—and hopefully there won't be."

Molly rolled her eyes. "It's not that bad," she said.

"The bands perform on a barge, and the audience listens from the dock. For the past couple years, the Butchers were the only band there, because the Butchers were literally *the only band* in school."

"Ivan Brink got the Undead Fainting Goats together," Edwin pointed out.

"The little vampire kid?" I said. "The one who faints on purpose all the time?"

"That's him," said Edwin. "Anyway, they formed in September and broke up in October. Basically, everyone's too terrified of the Butcher to even *have* a band. But this year, the Dweebs will break that streak."

"We'll sort of be the warm-up band," said Molly.

I rolled my eyes. "That sucks."

"Yeah?" she said. "You got any better gigs lined up, rock star?"

"No." She had a point. "But wait—how'd we even get invited?"

"Turns out Gerald's good for *something*," said Molly.

That hung in the air for a second.

What the heck? Why was the Butcher help-  ing us? And, if Molly hated Gerald so much, why did she even hang around with him? I didn't say anything, but Edwin could apparently read my mind.

"I think new kid is wondering something," he said matter-of-factly to Molly. "Namely, if you *hate* the Butcher so much . . ."

"Tell new kid that Gerald's not so bad, once you get to know him," she said simply.

"New kid thinks that's what they all say," said Edwin. "But to his way of thinking, the Butcher gets worse and worse the *more* you get to know him."

Edwin had read my mind again.

"Okay," said Molly. "I've got to get going. I have to study. We can't all be super-geniuses."

So that was how it was: I liked Molly, and Molly liked to tease me. The more she teased, the more I liked her. The more I liked her, the more I pretended I didn't. And the more I pretended, the more she teased. We were doing some kind of crazy, circular dance . . . and I was getting dizzy.

The reason the whole thing was so idiotic and complicated was, of course, the Butcher. He apparently had some mysterious redeeming quality that only Molly could detect. Meanwhile, he hated me and I hated him. He got us the gig, but he wanted to kill me. Nice.

"So, when is this whole dock thing, anyway?" I asked.

"April first, a Saturday. The first day of spring break," said Molly, grabbing her soggy T-shirt from the counter.

"Makes sense—April Fool's," said Edwin. "We're gonna need more than just a song or two." He turned to me. "Better get writing, Henry Wadsworth Songfellow."

SIREN

Molly and I left the barbershop together.

"Where do you live, anyway?" she asked.

"Over near the Big M Market. Really close to school, actually."

"My house is on the way," she said.

We walked along, and she brought up English class again.

"I've never seen one ounce of humanity leak out of Danderbrook before," she said. "You made her gush."

"Oh, come on," I said. "It was no big deal."

"No big deal? You defrosted that woman."

Molly went on and on about how incredible it was. The more she talked, the more I worried. What if the Butcher came strolling by? What if he found out what had happened today? The laughing, the teasing, the wet T-shirt. What if I wasn't all that good at hiding my feelings for Molly? What if it was written all over my face? I was shivering a bit, and even though the sun was going

95

down and I was a little cold without my sweatshirt, it was partly because I was just plain nervous walking down the street with Molly.

When we arrived at her house, she opened the door and asked me to come in.

I wanted to. "Nah, I can't. I gotta go."

"Come on, T. S. Smelliot," she said. "We can do our homework together." Somehow, I never thought I'd like being called T. S. Smelliot. But I did.

I *really* wanted to. "Maybe next time."

"My parents are out, so they won't be bugging us."

Okay, this was torture. And it reminded me of something. The year before, I'd had to read *The Odyssey*. Well, part of it. I remembered the beautiful Sirens, whose songs lured sailors to their doom. Now I was one of those sailors getting trapped by a beautiful girl. Except *I* was the one who was attracting *her* with songs. Unintentionally. Okay, maybe intentionally.

I wanted Molly, and didn't want her. The two ideas were battling in my brain. Winning equaled doom, at the hands of one Gerald "the Butcher" Boggs.

"Listen, Molly," I said. I took a deep breath. "What's the deal with you and Gerald, anyway?"

"I don't know," she said, shrugging her shoulders. I thought I detected a flash of embarrassment on her face. "In seventh grade, everybody seemed to think we were the perfect couple, you know? And he's exciting to watch on the football field. You kind of fall for those fairy tales."

"You couldn't possibly see the Butcher as a handsome prince," I said, trying not to gag.

Molly thought for a minute. "Well, he is handsome."

"Are you serious?" *Give me a break.*

"Okay, you're not a girl. Plus, I've known him for a long time. He used to be nicer. He kind of reminds me of my brother. And he's not a moron, you know. He's actually pretty smart." She sounded a little defensive about that part. She paused to think for a moment, like she was working it out for herself. "I don't know, it took him a while to become what he is today. His parents are completely nuts. His dad is a jerk, never around. And his mom is some sort of zombie society lady, who cares more about her clothes and furniture than Gerald."

I guess it sort of made sense, but Molly sounded a little like a lawyer making excuses for an obviously guilty client.

"It still doesn't explain why you hang around with him," I pointed out.

"Well, some things are hard to explain," she said. "Anyway, do you want this?"

She threw the rolled-up Mad Manny T-shirt at me.

"Why? You look great in it. You had it on the first time I saw you." Maybe I shouldn't have said that. Was that creepy?

"I know," she said. "It was my brother's, but he outgrew it. I was only wearing it because I miss him now that he's away at college." She looked a little sad. "But you should wear it when the Dweebs play."

"Swing on down to Guitar Jungle," I called — in a very good Mad Manny voice, if I do say so myself.

"It'll be nice and tight on you. Rock-band tight," Molly said. "I can't think of a better shirt for the leader of a band called the Amazing Dweebs."

She had a point. The shirt was amazing, and very dweeby. Of course, there'd be a dangerous downside if the Butcher saw me in it.

"And I'll keep your sweatshirt," she added, smiling.

"Really?" What was Molly doing? What was she trying to say? "Okay," I continued, tucking the Mad Manny shirt under my arm. "But I really gotta go now."

I turned . . . and tripped over a rose bush. I pulled a ridiculous ballet move, trying to avoid falling. But I landed flat on my face in the grass, anyway.

Talk about a dweeb. I had to cover for it, somehow.

"Ta-da!" I said, leaping back up.

Molly laughed, and I got the impression it was mostly *with* me, not *at* me. "See you later, Lord of the Dance," she said, closing the door.

On the way home, I wrote a song in my head.

SONG #4
TWO IDEAS
By Davis Delaware

Two ideas fight it out,
Within the wrinkles of my brain.
A mighty microscopic bout,
Fifteen rounds of love and pain.

Left brain, right brain, cerebellum,
Cerebral cortex, frontal lobe,
Love 'em, lose 'em, shuck 'em, shell 'em,
Same old story 'round the globe.

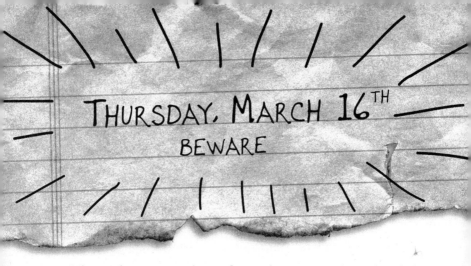

THURSDAY, MARCH 16TH
BEWARE

Three things stand out from this particular school day:

1.) I got to my locker in the morning and there, written on a yellow Post-it, were the words "DEAD DWEEB." The fact that it was scrawled in bloodred marker made the message even clearer. I grabbed it, crumpled it up, and stuck it in my pocket.

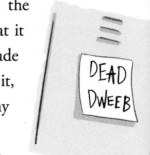

2.) At the end of the day, I stopped at my locker again. The same words — but much bigger letters — were scratched into the paint of the locker door.

3.) Hoo boy.

YES

I had originally planned a battle royal with Dad after school over the whole karate thing. I was sure I could talk him out of it. But the more I imagined that maniac Gerald lurking around and threatening me, the more I thought that maybe learning a little self-defense wasn't such a bad idea.

Dad was sitting on the couch after dinner, reading the newspaper.

"You know," I said, "I think I might be up for that karate business."

He looked surprised. "Well . . . I'm glad you're finally being a little sensible about this. It certainly couldn't hurt to meet a few more kids."

"Right," I said.

"Good," Dad said, getting up. "Because I went and got you a gi today." He opened his briefcase and pulled out a tightly shrink-wrapped karate outfit.

I opened it, and a starched and folded white belt fell

on the floor. I shook out the gi, but its large square-ish top and bottom still had a grid of fold lines across it. "I'm gonna look like a waffle in this."

"Hang it up," he said. "It'll be fine for your first class tomorrow. Three o'clock—don't be late. And please don't quit." Dad turned back to his newspaper.

What did he mean, "don't quit"? The only thing I could remember ever quitting was Boy Scouts after two weeks when I was eleven. Was it my fault that the Scout leader was a psycho drill sergeant who should have traded in his uniform for a straightjacket? Sure, I quit right before Christmas, and Santa had apparently been all set to bring me every piece of new Scout paraphernalia his little elves could whip up. So the fat man was none too jolly about having to return everything and shop for all new crap late Christmas Eve. And I mean crap. The only place open was the 24-hour pharmacy. Merry Christmas to me.

"No, Dad . . . I won't quit."

I couldn't. Martial arts were going to save my life.

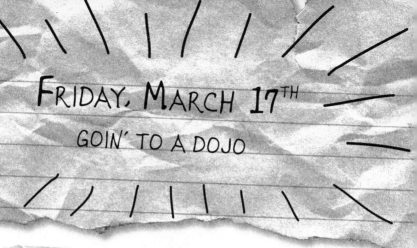

FRIDAY, MARCH 17TH

GOIN' TO A DOJO

SONG #5

CHOP 'TIL YOU DROP
By Davis Delaware

Chop 'til you drop like a big fruit salad,
Chop you, mince you, shred you, too,
Brag about it in this ballad,
Everybody knows it's true.

Chop 'til you drop down a drain to nowhere,
Slice you, dice you, flush you, too,
Through the sewer, then you'll go where
Fishes swim in fishy poo.

103

It was Saint Patrick's Day and I didn't wear anything green. So what, right? Okay, I had never heard of this quaint tradition, but apparently in this insane school, people pinch you for that. With my newfound poetry celebrity, even people I didn't know were pinching me, or at least trying to. Mrs. Toople got me three times. Molly got me once—the highlight of the festivities. I was afraid the Butcher would try to pinch my ear off again, but I successfully avoided close proximity. Luckily, we didn't have gym that day.

Mostly, I was thinking about karate. I'd pretty much decided that it was my ticket to a fear-free life. I knew I'd never be able to beat up the Butcher, but if I learned the basics, maybe I could at least keep him from annihilating me.

The dojo wasn't too far away, but in order to make it on time, I would really have to race from my last class to my locker, and out the door. As the last bell rang and I bolted from my seat, Mr. Waverton, my history teacher, appeared in front of me, blocking my way.

"What's this I hear about someone being the new poet laureate of Woodrow Wilson?"

"Who, me? No, no, I don't know anything about poetry," I said, moving from side to side, trying to make my way past him.

"That's not what I hear, Delaware," he said, moving

with me, like he was covering me in a full-court press.

"Well, I'm afraid it's true, Mr. Waverton," I said, finally elbowing my way past him and through the crowd of students. "Sorry, I've gotta get going."

Not a chance. There were the six or seven kids swarming near my locker, just wanting to talk. Suddenly, I was someone people wanted to talk to.

Ivan Brink, the chubby little fainting vampire kid, came up to me. He seemed to have actual fangs. His hair was jet-black. His face was chalk white. He had painted one red teardrop dripping from his eye. He wore black high-water pants that exposed more than two inches of pale, hairless ankle above his black socks and shoes. I guess he wasn't a fan of the logo on his black polo shirt, because there was a gaping hole where the cute little crocodile or penguin or whatever used to be.

"Hey, Dela-who, why no green?" he whispered in his high-pitched vampire voice. I guess he thought "Dela-who" was hilarious. I thought it was hilarious that a guy who, as always, was all in black, was suddenly concerned about me not wearing green. He smiled and

continued, "I loved that stuff in your poem about lying in a pool of blood. What was that again?"

"I can't really remember," I said.

"That's cool, Dela-who. Hey, I hear you're playing Rock Around the Dock? And you're in some band called the Dweebs with Molly?"

"Yeah," said another kid I'd never seen before. "Are you going out with her or something?"

"What? No!" I said, looking around to make sure the Butcher wasn't nearby. "Definitely not."

"Well, the blood thing was cool, anyway," said Ivan. He paused for a minute, like he was thinking of something else to say. I was never going to get to karate on time. "Hey, wanna see me pass out?" Ivan was known for holding his breath until he fainted.

"You know," I said, "I'm no doctor, but that *might* not be good for you." This procedure required an assistant to give him a barrel hug at just the right moment. Some kids were willing to do it because it was dramatic. I was horrified. And in a hurry.

I turned away and walked straight into three cute cheerleader types, one of whom immediately pinched me.

"Ha, forgot to wear green! Hey, I heard you wrote some bizarre poem about kids melting or something?" said the pincher, clearly the leader of the trio. A few days ago she wouldn't have looked at me twice. Or even once.

That felt good. And weird.

"No . . . well, sort of . . ."

"So, you're playing down at the dock with Molly? Are you two an item now?" She said it like Molly was a celebrity, which she kind of was at Wilson.

"No! Jeez! Why does everyone keep asking me that? Never mind . . . I gotta go." I turned and headed for the door.

Then—I couldn't believe it—the *principal* called out to me.

"Mr. Delaware!" said Mr. Rigo. "Hold on there a second!"

Good lord, what *now*?

"I just want to say how pleased I am to hear that you're acclimating to Woodrow Wilson so well. I was a little worried about a student coming in so late in the year, but you seem to be doing just swimmingly." He patted me on the shoulder. He was big on shoulder patting.

"Yes, Mr. Rigo," I said, slowly walking away from him backward, trying to get the heck out of there.

"I see that you hit it off with Gerald Boggs. It was nice that he was making you feel welcome in the cafeteria the other day. You'd be surprised—he doesn't get along with every student. I've known him for a long time. I play golf with his dad."

"Huh," I said, desperately trying not to roll my eyes. "Isn't that interesting?"

"Yes, well, I met him years ago at an Elks Club function. . . ."

Was he kidding? Now I had to hear the entire history of his deep bond with Gerald "the Butcher" Boggs's father? Didn't he realize that Gerald was a horrible human being and that, according to Molly, his father was even worse? This nonsense was coming from the principal of the school? The man who the parents of the community trusted to watch over and guide their beloved kiddies along the highways and byways of adolescence?

Rigo kept talking. He seemed to be suffering from Edwin-itis all of a sudden.

But if he was Edwin, I could have just told him to shut up. Instead, I had to stand around and listen.

By the time I finally got out of there, I was already twenty minutes late for karate. I ran all ten blocks to Jo-Jo's Dojo. (This was harder than it sounds, because my backpack was overstuffed with my gi and about fifty pounds of books.)

When I walked through the door, I was amazed. Tons of kids were screaming and chopping the air. I didn't know anything about it, other than the fact that it looked cool and maybe it was my salvation.

I could see Sensei Jo-Jo demonstrating some moves

to a bunch of serious-looking gi-wearing guys and girls, from kindergarteners through twelfth graders or higher. He was a very skinny white guy with a wispy beard—nothing like what I'd expected. He looked like a hippie version of Uncle Sam.

And that's when it hit me. And I don't mean hit me, like I realized something. No, something actually hit me. Something huge. It felt like a couch or maybe a house had landed on me. This was turning into the unluckiest St. Patrick's Day ever.

I slammed onto the hardwood floor. Man, did that hurt. My head was spinning. As I struggled to get out from under whatever had landed on me, I realized it was a human. A very large human.

"Sorry, dweeb," said a familiar voice. "Didn't see you there."

Seriously? Was the Butcher *everywhere*?

I had no idea he did karate. Football, wrestling, karate . . . I guess he naturally gravitated to any activity that gave him the opportunity to pound on people. My entire self-preservation plan swirled down the drain.

I looked up at the big hulk and all the other gi-wearers gathered around.

The Butcher turned to the sensei. "Very sorry, Sensei Jo-Jo. I just didn't expect this new, inexperienced student to be loitering right in the way there. He was late, and wearing shoes on the dojo floor. Everyone knows he should have been kneeling in the back, awaiting your permission to join the group."

Gerald had amazingly good manners all of a sudden.

Sensei Jo-Jo spoke to me: "Name?"

"Delaware."

"No, I asked your *name*. But I'm from Delaware, too. What part?"

"No . . . not . . . I'm . . . ouch . . ." Shoulder throbbing, head pounding, having trouble talking.

"Never mind," said the sensei. "Since you are so late, you cannot participate. Please watch from the gallery above. Next time, you must arrive fifteen minutes early for warm-up."

How was I supposed to know that?

The Butcher leaned close and smiled like a spider to

a fly. "The dweeb will cry . . . and the dweeb will die," he whispered.

The joke was on him. He might kill me, but he'd never make me cry.

The other students loaded me up with what now seemed like my two-hundred-pound backpack, and I climbed the wobbly stairs to the gallery—a long, thin balcony where parents and little siblings sat to watch the practice. It was hot and crowded. I squeezed in between a couple of snot-nosed brothers who, inspired by what was going on below, beat on each other the entire time. When I call them "snot-nosed," it's not just an insult, it's an accurate description. And believe me, when two rug rats wrestle, they don't keep their noses to themselves. Plus, they noticed I wasn't wearing green, and the pinching started again.

It was immediately obvious that Gerald "the Butcher" Boggs was king of Karate Town. He could have taken on all the other kids at once. He made eye contact with me before pummeling his sparring partner with a quick flurry of kicks and chops, and then flashed me a freaky evil smile. The partner looked terrified, but he had no idea how good he had it. He was just a temporary stand-in for the Butcher's real punching bag.

So much for karate. In retrospect, I was lucky to be late. Maybe I could just be late *every* Friday. But I knew my dad would find out, and he was so excited about the whole martial-arts-friend-finding scheme. "It certainly couldn't hurt," he'd said.

Little did he know that he had enrolled me in the *house* of hurt, the parlor of pain — the dojo of death.

SATURDAY, MARCH 18TH
THE GLOSSARY OF GOONS

Dad was still at work when I went to sleep that night, and he left early the next morning. I think he was working so much to make a good impression at his new job. So he wasn't around even if I'd wanted to talk about what had happened that day, but I decided that the whole karate nightmare was one more thing I wouldn't be filling him in on. He was on a need-to-know basis, and, as far I was concerned, he didn't need to know.

I definitely didn't want to tell him the truth about the Butcher. Parents always get all worked up about "getting to the bottom" of stuff like that. Phone calls, interrogations, powwows, and punishments never solve anything. They just make bad situations worse. Different, but worse.

So, now I was keeping good *and* bad news from my dad. If anything totally neutral ever happened, he would be the first to hear about it.

I was on my own for lunch. I looked in the fridge

and found a small, foil-wrapped something that turned out to be the final remains of the spaghetti brains. I rewrapped it and stuck it way in the back of the fridge, behind the baking soda and the maraschino cherries. No-man's land, where maybe Dad would forget about it.

Instead of subjecting myself to that, I decided to make what I usually make when I'm alone — PBJB&A, the food of the gods: peanut butter, jam, banana, and apple on toast. Jam, not jelly. And it has to be toast. Hot peanut-butter-jam-banana-apple pie. Load it up and it runs like sweet lava.

I've experimented with tons of variations on peanut butter sandwiches. I picked up where George Washington Carver left off. PBJB&A is by far the best. You have to gulp lots of milk straight from the carton, too. Open it on the open-other-side side and re-close carefully, so that lip prints go unde-tected. Eat leaning over the sink. Hold

the concoction in one hand, catch drips with the other.

When the feast is over — in, say, fifteen seconds — just lick your fingers and arms, rinse the rest down the drain, and go. No fuss, no muss, no more hunger.

I went to my room and got back to work.

SONG #6
COUNTDOWN
By Davis Delaware

FOUR, THREE, TWO, ONE...
Four, I'll draw a sketch of you,
Doodle 'til you're black and blue.
Three, I'll scribble out your eyes,
Add some maggots and some flies.
Two, then I'll erase your face,
You'll be gone without a trace.
One, I'll say a prayer that you
Rest in peace in doggy doo.

I drew a truly horrifying portrait of Gerald, melting like the Stay Puft Marshmallow Man on a huge s'more while the rest of the school sang around a roaring campfire. Sure, it was creepy and mean. But it wasn't for anyone to see but me. And it felt so good. I really got into the details: flaming sores, oozing infections, weird growths, bubbling blisters and bulges. Worms and insects crawled out of his eyes and ears. Smoke and pus erupted from his pores like teeny volcanoes. I drew more realistically than ever before, using the side of the pencil to shade every disgusting detail. I'd never had any actual drawing lessons, but I was figuring out how to use shadows to make something look 3-D. Maybe if I made it *look* real, it would *be* real.

There was something satisfying about being in complete control of this version of Gerald — how many pimples, how few teeth, how tiny a brain. In my notebooks, all those decisions were up to me. It gave me a strange sense of power.

That's when I got the idea for the Glossary of Goons, a dictionary for defining and categorizing some of the "favorite" characters in my life, on my own terms, for me — a committee of one. The first entry was, of course:

Gerald Boggs. *n.*
1. an idiot turd-faced jerk.
2. a scum-sucking pea-brain jerk.
3. a numbskull-loser pimple-eyed jerk.
4. get it? He's more than one kind of jerk.
5. jerkity-jerk-jerk-jerk.

I started thinking about all those other goons, creeps, cretins, and ninnies that hung around with Gerald. Actually, I didn't know much about them. They weren't in any of my classes or anything. So, I just made stuff up based on how they looked. You're not supposed to judge books by their covers, but it was obvious — these books were bad. It was even possible that their covers *covered up* some of their badness.

Anton Squilt. *n.*
1. an idiot turd-faced jerk worshipper.
2. an idiot turd-faced jerk butt-kisser.

squilt. *v.*
1. to worship and/or kiss the butt of an idiot turd-faced jerk.

KARL
KIDDER

Karl Kidder, n.
1. a drooler.
2. a heavy drooler.
3. the Niagara Falls of droolers.

Willard Gourdinski, n.
1. a nervous, hyper, sweaty, ferocious individual.
2. an individual who behaves as if he has a swarm of killer bees inside his head.
3. an individual who is rumored to literally have a swarm of killer bees inside his head.

WILLARD
GOURDINS

gourdinski, v.
1. to ski erratically, as if the skier has a swarm of killer bees inside his head.

I had PBJB&A for dinner, too. I'd be happy to eat it three times a day, seven days a week. It beat leftover spaghetti brains and shaky cheese, anyway. Afterward, there wasn't much peanut butter left, so I just used a spoon and finished off the jar. I squirted in about a pint of chocolate syrup, too. Hey, it was dessert.

As the day went on, I added a bunch more entries to the Glossary of Goons and wrote a song in honor of all of them.

SONG #7
THAT'S RIGHT, YOU HEARD ME RIGHT!

By Davis Delaware

Big fat bozo, skinny kid smart,
Rich kid, poor kid, smelly dumb fart.
Jerks and jokers come in all sizes,
Some you know, and some surprises.
From dawn to noon to dead of night,
The world's full of blockheads — That's
right, you heard me right!

119

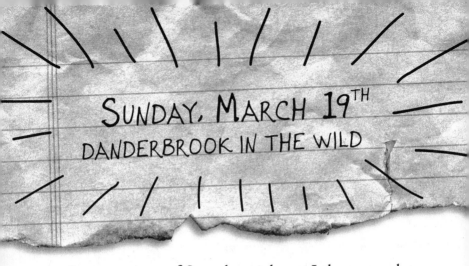

SUNDAY, MARCH 19TH
DANDERBROOK IN THE WILD

I was up most of Saturday night, so I slept super-late on Sunday. When I finally got up, I looked in the fridge. It wasn't a pretty sight now that the peanut butter was gone. It was like a ghost town in there. I think I saw a tumbleweed roll by in the vegetable drawer.

Dad had left me some cash in an envelope, so I headed out for the Big M. It was a discount supermarket, the closest place. They had regular stuff, but the peanut butter was very irregular. There were only two choices.

One was the bad hippie kind. I've got nothing against all-natural, and I don't even care if I have to mix it up. Don't get me wrong, there are okay hippie kinds of peanut butter. But some brands—and this looked like one of them—are almost impossible to mix. It's like a big brown peanut boulder submerged in grease. And after it's refrigerated, the grease hardens. Yum. It takes all the fun out of peanut butter. And that's saying a lot.

The other kind they had was the super-pale processed

stuff that barely even tastes like peanuts. Peanuts are the fourth ingredient on the label. This tastes like pure lard, with just a hint o' peanut. A subtle essence of legume.

Anyway, I was standing in the aisle, holding up the hippie peanut butter and trying to decide if I was up to the challenge, when someone called my name.

"Davis? Davis Delaware?"

And there was Miss Danderbrook, out in the real world. It's always shocking to see teachers removed from their natural habitat. Miss Danderbrook was wearing a T-shirt, shorts, and flip-flops. It wasn't even that warm outside.

"How's your weekend going, Davis?"

"Pretty good," I said. "Nice flip . . . flops?" I was so distracted by her outfit, I had trouble talking. She looked about ten years younger. I wondered if I should introduce her to my dad.

"Thanks," she said. "By the way, the poetry club magazine is coming out this week. There will be a release party on Wednesday after school. I think you'll be pleased. You're featured on the cover."

"Wow, a poetry cover boy," I said, feeling embarrassed, but proud. "Okay, I'll see you then, I guess."

"Well, I'll see you tomorrow in class, too."

"Oh, right, tomorrow." Duh.

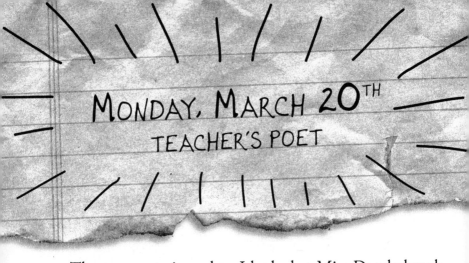

The next morning when I looked at Miss Danderbrook in class, I couldn't stop thinking about the flip-flops. I was kind of shocked at how much more human she seemed all of a sudden.

She divided the class into small groups to work more on poetry—except me. She let me sit at my desk by myself, like I was some sort of poet-in-residence or something. I was definitely reaping the rewards of my new Teacher's Pet status.

After a while, Danderbrook asked me to read another poem. "Is there something special you've been working on that you'd like to share?" she asked.

I pulled out my notebook and flipped to a song that was definitely special. Of course, I recited it as a poem again . . . with an extra helping of dramatic energy. I stood up.

"Full of Bleep!" I shouted, my voiced laced with anger and attitude. The title alone made everyone jump,

including Miss Danderbrook, who accidentally threw her pencil into the air. I woke them all from their first-period siesta. I really cranked it up, like a beatnik poet from an old movie. I tilted my head back and let 'er rip:

Hey, you, you're such a jerk!

(I pointed at an imaginary person out in front of me somewhere. One girl thought I meant her, and she nearly fell off her chair.)

Yeah, you, you're such a creep!

(I swung my arm around and jabbed my finger toward another invisible target of my rage.)

Hey, you, your head don't work!

(I pointed to my head.)

Yeah, you, you're full of bleep!

(Finger straight up in the air.)

By the time I got to the "Full of bleep" line, I could tell it was a hit. I kept going, and every time I got to the end of another stanza, the students joined in: *Yeah, you, you're full of bleep!* It actually got pretty rowdy for an English class.

When it was over, Danderbrook quieted everyone down. I don't think she appreciated this poem as much as the melting-clock one, but at this point she was a Davis Delaware fan. She asked me to move around the room to help her critique the poems of other students. I just told everyone their work was stunning, groundbreaking, whatever.

Molly was amused: "Thanks for your valuable assistance, Edgar Allan Poetry."

Edwin seemed irritated: "Quoth me: 'Nevermore.'"

For the rest of the day, I couldn't stop thinking about songs or poems or whatever they were. I was in the zone. People basically had to yell at me to make contact: *Hello!*

Yoo-hoo! Anybody home, poetry man? All the positive feedback I'd been getting was inspiring me to put as much down on paper as I could, as fast as possible.

Whenever I got a minute, I scribbled in a notebook. If I didn't have one handy, I scribbled on the back of a math test, or a napkin, or my arm. I was pretty sure I wasn't a great writer or artist. And I was positive that I was a horrible musician. But I guess I just didn't care about that. I was obsessed.

TUESDAY, MARCH 21ST
SHETTLE

Mr. Shettle seemed to hate all kids, but he had some kind of rare species of bug up his butt about me. I guess it was because I was new meat. He was bored with the other kids he'd been making fun of forever, and I gave him an opportunity to try out new material.

The bell rang as I ran into the gym. I was literally three seconds late.

"Delaware!" Shettle howled. "You're crazy if you think you can waltz in late!"

"Well, you're crazy if you think this is a waltz," I said, whipping out a dance move that could only be described as crazy. I think poetry fame had gone to my head.

I got too big of a laugh.

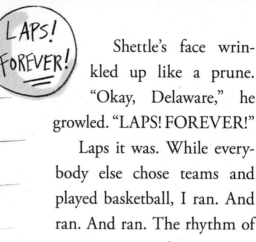

Shettle's face wrinkled up like a prune. "Okay, Delaware," he growled. "LAPS! FOREVER!"

Laps it was. While everybody else chose teams and played basketball, I ran. And ran. And ran. The rhythm of running conjured up a song in my head. I sort of whispered it under my breath, along with the slap-slap-slapping of my sneakers on the hardwood floor:

Shettle, Shettle, wins the medal.
He's as dumb as teachers get-tle.
If your head is made of lumber,
You are smarter, Shettle's dumb-ber.

Okay, yeah, it was a silly song. But the mispronunciation of "dumber" cracked me up. I guess because I was singing it about Shettle, right there in Shettle's class, it seemed like a funny combination of dangerous and ridiculous. I started laughing to myself.

Before long, the Butcher and Shettle noticed.

Gerald must have thought that I was laughing at *him*, because every time he got the basketball he threw it as hard as he could at me, as if I was a duck in a shooting gallery. It was like the extreme dodgeball game from the other week had never ended. Gerald pretended to be going for the basket or passing to a teammate, but it was obvious that he was aiming for my legs, trying to trip me up, hoping I'd land on my head. Shettle totally knew what was going on, but I think he was happy to have the Butcher do his dirty work for him.

I got hit a few times, nothing too bad. I decided to ham up the shooting-gallery theme a bit—striking silly duck poses in midair and even quacking a few times. Why not? In a lot of ways, this was better than actually playing basketball with the Butcher. I'm sure he could have easily found a way to elbow me in the ribs or the eye or the nose, or flatten me like a pancake.

I had become the Butcher's favorite target, in and out of gym class. Quite the claim to fame.

Lucky me.

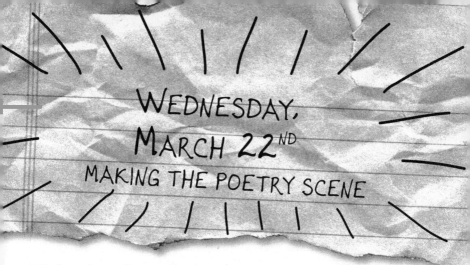

WEDNESDAY, MARCH 22ND
MAKING THE POETRY SCENE

Wednesday after school was the poetry club magazine release party. They held it in Miss Danderbrook's classroom, but there were poets from ninth through twelfth grades included—mostly girls. Molly was there. The only other boy was Ivan Brink, everyone's favorite chunky fainting-goat vampire freak.

"Good to see you, Ivan," I overheard Molly say as I walked in the door. "Promise me you won't pass out on the cheese and crackers."

"I promise," he said, smiling proudly. Everyone likes to be known for something.

Danderbrook served sparkling apple cider in plastic champagne glasses. There was a stack of magazines on the table, and all the contributors were supposed to autograph the title pages. The cover had a black-and-white reproduction of Salvador Dalí's melty-clock painting and the headline read, *"Watch the Melting Clock: Meditations on Time* by Davis Delaware and the rest of the Woodrow

Wilson Poetry Club." Even though Danderbrook had warned me, I was kind of embarrassed to get top billing like that.

Molly walked up to me. "So, how's it feel to be Super Poetry Dude?" she asked.

"The thrill of a lifetime," I said in an un-thrilled monotone.

"Somebody's not so pleased," said Molly, motioning with her eyes at a girl across the room. "That's Charlotte Carlotta, a senior. She's sort of the poster girl for poetry club."

Was she ever: Emily Dickinson ribbon around her neck, Sylvia Plath T-shirt, Dylan Thomas hoodie.

Where the heck did she get all that stuff? Poetry-R-Us?

It wasn't long before she wandered over. "So, I assume you were in the poetry club back in Delaware?" she asked, sipping her cider . . . pinkie out.

"No, not really," I said. I had decided to just let people think I was from Delaware. It wasn't worth correcting them.

"Oh," she said, "because I was kind of surprised that Miss Danderbrook decided to put you on the cover and everything. You're a *beginner*, and a few of us are *obviously* so much more *advanced*. I mean, some of these kids shouldn't even be in the magazine. But I, for one, was kind of disappointed about the cover especially, because it just didn't seem fair . . . you know?"

I couldn't believe my ears. This was the kind of smart girl who gave smart girls a bad name.

"Oh, yeah, Charlotte, I can see why you would feel that way," Molly chimed in, raising an eyebrow at me. "But it's just that there wasn't a poetry club in Davis's old school. He's kind of beyond that, anyway. He's already published . . . professionally, I mean. Plus, he was Delaware All-State Poetry Champ three years running."

What a girl.

"Wow," gasped Charlotte, causing a small trickle of apple cider to dribble down her chin, which she quickly dabbed with a napkin. "I don't think we even *have* statewide poetry competitions here in New York."

"Delaware has always been very advanced, poetry-wise," I said. "God, I miss the First State. They call it that because it was the first state to ratify the Constitution. They're first in poetry, too. It's one of their major exports."

"I hope to move there one day," Molly said wistfully. "Do you know the state song, Davis?"

"Do I know the state song?" I asked in fake disbelief. "I only sang it at last year's all-state's." Molly was gonna love this.

"Oh, Delaware.
Oh, Delaware,
Your poetry and wonder.
Your ocean views and bays and boats,
Your lightning and your thunder.
When I'm away, I'm feeling blue,
I miss your rhymes, your meter, too. . . ."

"I can't remember the rest, but you get the idea."

Molly clapped softly, politely, like little old ladies do at fancy recitals. She also pretended to wipe a tear from her eye. Nice touch.

"So," said Charlotte, eyeing me suspiciously, "where exactly have you been published?"

"Where *hasn't* he been published is more like it," said Molly.

I covered my mouth to hide the smile that was threatening to burst into a laugh.

"Have you heard of *New Yorker* magazine?" I said. I was really going overboard here. Something about the way she'd said "beginner" and "obviously" and "advanced" got to me. She seemed like a bully—the Butcher of poetry.

Charlotte nodded, wide-eyed. It was like she'd just met a movie star. "'Watch the Melting Clock' is fairly interesting," she said. It sounded like it hurt her to force the words out.

"Thanks. That means a lot coming from you."

"To Davis Delaware!" Molly cried, lifting her glass.

"Oh, please," I said. "I'm blushing."

"By all means," said Charlotte. "To Davis Delaware!"

"Cheers!" We all clinked glasses.

"Cheers!" said Miss Danderbrook from across the room.

In the silence that followed, Ivan Brink spoke up. "I'm thinking of getting a tattoo on my chest of one of those melting clocks . . . in a pool of blood."

Everyone stared at Ivan for a minute. But there was nothing to say.

"My parents subscribe to the *New Yorker*," Charlotte said, turning back to me. "I'll be sure to look for your work."

Later, I saw her whispering to her friends, spreading the news about the new kid who was a published poet.

I felt a little bad about all the lying—but not really. Goofing around with Molly was too much fun.

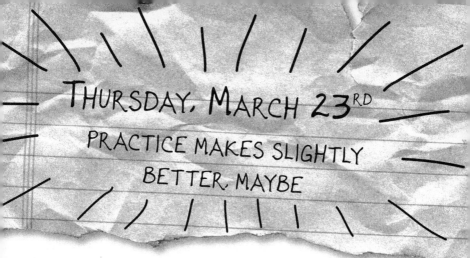

THURSDAY, MARCH 23RD
PRACTICE MAKES SLIGHTLY BETTER, MAYBE

The next day after school, I headed over to the barber-shop for band practice. I was all ready to teach Molly and Edwin "That's Right, You Heard Me Right!" I'd written another verse:

Big bad dumbbell, crazy little nut,
Athlete, mathlete, muscles, or gut.
Jerks and jokers all around you,
Some will tease you, others pound you.
From dawn to noon to dead of night,
The world's full of blockheads —
That's right, you heard me right!

Molly listened for a bit, and then joined in with harmony. It actually wasn't too bad. It was all starting to sound less like noise, and more like noisy music. Plus, singing harmony with a girl is sort of an intimate thing. It felt like the closest thing to kissing without actually kissing. Another feeling I would have to keep to myself.

Practice flew by.

Afterward, Molly asked what I was doing over the weekend.

"I don't know. . . ." It was one thing to see her at the barbershop, but running around town together would look dangerously date-like to a certain jealous maniac.

"I've gotta go," Molly said, opening the barbershop door. "My dad's picking me up. Call me."

"What do you want me to call you?" Oof.

"Funny," she said, rolling her eyes as she walked away. "Just call me."

FRIDAY, MARCH 24ᵀᴴ
SPARKY

I got to my second karate class early after bolting out of school, and Sensei Jo-Jo directed me to the group I would be working with. I was a beginner, so I was stuck with a bunch of little kids. Hey, at least I wouldn't be working with the Butcher.

A ten-year-old yellow belt was the leader of our group. How humiliating. I towered over them all.

The yellow-belted munchkin looked at me. "Hi, I'm Sparky."

"You're kidding, right?" I asked.

"Kidding about what?" He was not amused.

"Never mind."

I was pretty sure I wasn't going to learn anything from Sparky that would help me defend myself against the Butcher.

Sparky stood up tall and looked me right in the belly button. "Okay, Davis. Do you know the ethics chants?"

"Umm . . . no," I said. "This is my first day."

Another, even tinier kid glanced up at me and rolled his eyes.

Just then, the Butcher walked in and immediately approached the sensei. I couldn't hear what the Butcher was saying, but it was obvious from his hand gestures that he wanted to take over as leader of my group. The sensei shook his head no and pointed to Sparky. The Butcher grimaced and joined another group across the room.

I guess he couldn't bully Sensei Jo-Jo.

Sparky spoke to the tinier kid: "Joey, could you instruct our beginner?"

Oh, great. I'd been passed off to the mini-munchkin.

"Sure," squeaked Joey, turning to me. "The ethics chants. Learn them, love them, live them:

"To strive for the perfection of character.
To follow the paths of truth.
To foster a spirit of effort.
To honor the principles of etiquette.
To guard against impetuous courage."

"Okay, got it," I said, wondering which of these things the Butcher truly honored. I thought about how he'd probably added a few of his own:

> *To throttle first, ask questions later.*
> *To worship the way of the fist.*
> *To hold ever-sacred and dispense with*
>   *extreme prejudice the hair-smooth move.*

Joey looked at me and spoke like I was very, very slow: "The ethics chants. Learn them, love them, live them."

"Yes, master, you mentioned that, master," I said with a trace of Frankenstein in my voice.

Sparky looked over at me disapprovingly. Joey rolled his eyes again. Even mini-munchkin was embarrassed to be working with me.

"Okay," he said, "now we face each other."

Oh, brother. Joey was about two feet tall. He showed me the stretching exercises, and I followed along as best I could. I knew how to count a bit in Japanese — okay, from watching Sesame Street — so at least I got that part right.

Ichi! Ni! San! Shi! Go! Roku!

Ichi! Ni! San! Shi! Go! Roku!

We repeated that about a million times while we stretched.

Then we sparred a bit. Of course, I had no idea what I was doing. Thankfully, as hard as he tried — and he really tried hard — Joey couldn't beat me up or anything.

I had so much reach on him, I just kept my arms out and he couldn't get close. But I wasn't learning squat.

The Butcher spent the entire class glaring at me. This was an exercise in frustration for him. He wanted to get to me, but he couldn't. The sensei was watching everything like a hawk. And when the class ended, he called the Butcher over.

"Just a moment, Sensei Jo-Jo," said the Butcher. He crossed the room quickly and put his arm around me, like he was giving me counsel. He made karate chops with one hand, to make it look like he was helping me out. But here's what he said under his breath:

"Listen, dweeb. You'd better stop trying to steal my girlfriend—"

"I'm *not*," I interrupted.

"Liar," he continued. "And just in case you think you're safe . . . you're not safe. Sometime this weekend, when you least expect it, when I know you're alone, when Daddy isn't there to protect you, Mr. Fist is going to pay you a little visit." He showed me Mr. Fist. Oh, boy. "And Mr. Fist will meet Miss Face . . ." He pointed to my face—*Miss* Face, for some reason. My face was female

MR. FIST!

all of a sudden. "And when they meet, it ain't gonna be pretty."

Did he get this from a bad movie or something? The sensei called him over again, and as soon as the Butcher walked away, I got out of there. Dad was waiting out front in the car. I didn't even know he was coming, but I was glad to see him. I had something to tell him.

"Hey, how'd it go?" he asked as I got in.

"Good, good," I said. "Meeting lots of kids. Hey, Dad, you know how you wanted to go camping and fishing this weekend? Let's do it."

"Really?" he said, smiling. First I'd agreed to karate, and now this. I was suddenly the Best Kid Ever. "Let's load up the car and get out of here first thing in the morning. I love this spur-of-the-moment kind of thing."

He was overjoyed that I wanted to spend quality time with him, but really I just wanted to be out of town when Mr. Fist dropped by. As dumb as the Butcher's threats sounded, I knew they would feel very real to Miss Face.

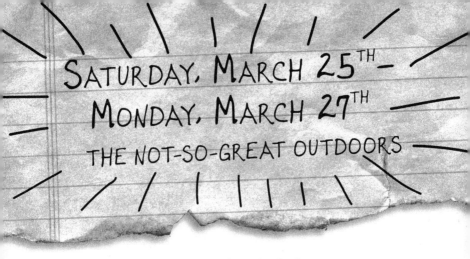

SATURDAY, MARCH 25TH – MONDAY, MARCH 27TH
THE NOT-SO-GREAT OUTDOORS

Camping turned out to be a bad idea.

First, there were hours and hours of really, really, really boring car ride. Unfortunately, I forgot to bring any music along. Dad listened to some kind of business talk-radio show for a while until I pleaded with him to turn it off.

"So, all in all," said Dad, ignoring my pleas, "how's life for Davis Delaware?"

"Not too bad, Dad. You don't have to worry about me." I knew he was trying to draw me out and have some kind of heart-to-heart, but I wasn't in the mood.

When we finally got to the camping area that Dad had researched in some book, it was completely dark. We had only brought one tiny flashlight. We started setting up our tent in what we soon found out was a swamp. Just getting the tent to stay up was hard enough, but doing it while swatting mosquitoes was hellish. It had been unseasonably warm for the last few weeks, and mosquito season was already in full swing. I'm not talking about a few mosquitoes, either. Nope, this was apparently the blood-sucking capital of the Adirondacks.

But the black flies were way worse. Those don't just make you itch, they do serious damage. I know that they probably don't actually have rows of razor-sharp teeth, but that's how it feels, like tiny flying sharks. They go for any area of exposed skin — ankles, wrists, neck, and face. Inside the ears. Your left eyelid.

So, the tent construction went something like:

"Insert into . . . ARGGGH!"

"Hammer that AHHHHHHH!"

"Pull that ACKKKKK! C'mon, my *right* eyelid, too?"

Then it started to rain.

Somehow we got the tent up and crawled inside. We zipped the mosquito-netted doorway closed and wriggled into our sleeping bags.

The tent had been the perfect size for the two of us when I was little, but not anymore. When you touch the inside of a tent when it's raining, you spring a little leak.

When your entire body is pushed up against it, you get a flood.

"Um, Noah?—I mean, Dad? Maybe we should have built an ark instead."

The good news was that the netting successfully shut the black flies out. The bad news? It did nothing to stop the mosquitoes. It was like some kind of medieval torture chamber in that tent. The buzzing in my ears was almost as bad as the bites. I zipped up the sleeping bag around my head, so that I was completely encased in it. But that was no help, either. It was like a bug-infested sarcophagus.

We'd brought books, and I had a notebook with me, but trying to read, write, or draw under those conditions was a total joke. We were afraid the flashlight batteries would die, anyway. So Dad and I spent the next few hours screaming and cursing in the dark—in pain, itchiness, and plain old mental anguish.

"ARRRGH!" *Swat!*

"AHHHHH!" *Swat! Swat!*

"DANG!" *Swat! Swat! Swat!* "Now my *bites* have bites!"

Somehow, we finally fell asleep.

Sunday was no better. It was still raining in the

morning. We tried fishing, but the swamp made that impossible. The lines got caught in the grass and weeds every two seconds, and the mosquitoes never let up.

By afternoon, the rain had stopped. But apparently, that was just the invitation the black flies were waiting for. Bug spray had absolutely no effect on them. It was like it *attracted* them.

"If we're the meat they crave," I said, swatting and wriggling like a crazy person, "the bug spray is their A1 Sauce."

"Yeah," said Dad, slapping at a fly, but hitting himself square in the face instead. "Maybe we should find another spot before we're their dessert, too."

We both smiled in spite of ourselves.

I thought about suggesting we find a hotel, but I knew Dad would be disappointed.

We packed up and hiked along until the swamp turned into a small river. A big, flat rock on the riverbank seemed like a decent place to stop. We pitched the tent there by tying the lines to nearby stones and, amazingly, it worked pretty well. The bug population was smaller there, too. Almost bearable.

"Hungry?" asked Dad, inspecting the tent proudly.

"Yup," I replied. "You didn't bring along any of that leftover spaghetti, did you? I mean, it was delish. Just wondering."

145

That got a laugh out of Dad. He was well aware of his shortcomings as a cook.

We built a fire and made our dinner: canned chili. It was incredibly good. We wolfed it down like . . . well, like wolves. It's the kind of thing that would taste terrible if you were eating it at your dining room table. But here, in the wilderness, it was a gourmet meal. The same goes for our dessert of toasted marshmallows, which I really hate raw. But somehow, melted, browned, or burned—heck, even dropped in the dirt and brushed off—as long as you're in the middle of nowhere, they are possibly the finest food known to man.

Then it started to rain again. Make that *pour*. Our fire was out in about ten seconds. We scrambled into the tent and into our sleeping bags.

"Pretty relaxing vacation, huh, Dad?"

"Yup. You know, ninety-nine point nine percent of the morons out there prefer four-star hotels."

"Total idiots," I said. "Nothing beats the great outdoors."

We listened to the rain for a while. The wind picked up, and it felt like the tent might take off like a kite.

"Your mom wasn't a big camper!" Dad said loudly out of the blue, over the howling wind and flapping tent.

"Yeah, I know!" I shouted. This was the first time he'd mentioned Mom in months.

"I miss her!"

"Me, too!"

Then the wind died down, and we didn't say anything for a while. The silence was broken by a gigantic thunderclap. Even though we were lying flat on our backs, we both jumped about a foot off the ground.

Then we cracked up.

"Yeah, sunny beaches are for suckers," I said.

"I know," he said. "Swimming, surfing . . . what a drag."

"You're telling me. I hate that whole *fun* thing."

"Yeah," Dad added. "Total misery is where it's at."

It had been a long time since I'd heard him laugh.

On Monday, more rain. An extended weekend of non-stop merriment. We finally gave up, rolled the tent into a big, muddy ball, and drove home. We pulled into our driveway around midnight.

By the time I got into my dry, warm bed, I had a slightly sore throat. Dad made me some hot lemonade with honey, which was something my mom used to do, so that was comforting.

I fell asleep before I drank it.

TUESDAY, MARCH 28TH – WEDNESDAY, MARCH 29TH
FEVER

Tuesday morning, Dad left early, and I went to school—but I shouldn't have.

I stumbled down the street, up the school steps, to my locker, and stared at those words scratched into the door's paint: "DEAD DWEEB." I realized that now there was also a crudely scratched skull above the words. Wonderful.

I felt dizzy and hot. I rested the side of my face against the cold metal locker door for a second. It was such a relief, I almost fell asleep standing up. Then I tried to open the lock. Nothing. I tried again. I think I might have been using the combination I'd had at my old school.

Finally, I gave up and just went to the nurse's office.

"What's the problem?" asked the nurse.

"I think my brain is broken," I said, slumping down in a chair.

"Excuse me?"

Then I tried to say, *I think I might have a fever*, but it came out "I" and then lots and lots of coughing. Followed by more coughing.

"Say ahhh," she instructed, sticking a thermometer in my mouth. I immediately coughed it across the room. It flew through the air like a tiny javelin and landed in the garbage can.

"Wow. That's the first time *that* ever happened," she said.

"Do I win something?" I croaked.

"Yes," she said, feeding me a spoonful of heavy-duty cough syrup that made me gag *and* cough.

Ivan Brink wandered in, looking a little loopy. "Hi, Dela-who-what-why."

"Ivan," said the nurse, "don't tell me you fainted again." She had no clue he was passing out on purpose.

He nodded and stuck his lower lip out, like he was feeling sorry for himself.

"You lie down on the couch," she said. "I'm calling your mother."

I expected Ivan to object with something like, *No, don't, I'll be okay.* It's what I would have done. But he didn't. He let her call, and I realized that was exactly what he wanted—a little attention.

I fell asleep in the chair, and the nurse woke me when Dad got there to pick me up. I didn't even realize she'd called him.

"So long, Ivan," I said, but he had conked out on the couch.

Dad took me home and forced me to get into bed.

"I have to get back to work," he said. "You just sleep, sleep, and sleep some more. Then, when you wake up, go back to sleep."

HALF-DEAD

The rest of the day and Wednesday were a feverish blur. Dad brought me to the doctor on Wednesday morning to get some medication, and then I just went back home and—surprise—slept for five more hours. Exciting stuff.

Wednesday night, I got a call from Edwin.

"Are you dead, or what?"

"I'm at least half-dead," I said.

"You sound *all* dead. Anyway, just in case you come back to life at some point, do you happen to recall what Saturday is?"

Of course I did. "Rock Around the freaking Dock."

"Bingo," Edwin said. "Are you gonna be better for that, or what?"

Of course I was. "Definitely, no question. Wouldn't miss it."

"You promise? I really don't wanna hear about how we chickened out for the next twenty years."

Tell me about it.

"Promise. And we need to have one more practice to work some stuff out," I said. "Do you wanna call Molly?" I expected him to complain about it: *Sure, no problem. I have no life. Nothing better to do with my time . . . blah, blah, blah.* But he didn't.

"Yes, boss," he said. I guess he really got that I was sick.

"Okay, Edwin, I'm going back to sleep now. See you tomorrow." I made a fake snoring sound and hung up. But I was snoring for real in about two seconds.

THURSDAY, MARCH 30TH
HOTTER

I woke up intending to go to school, but Dad came in early and took my temperature: 102.

"You're not going anywhere," he said.

"But, Dad, there's an important test today—"

"No way," he said.

So, he went to work, and I called Edwin to tell him that I wouldn't be at school, but that I'd meet them at the barbershop that afternoon. After a lot more sleep.

When I got to the barbershop, Edwin's dad and Furry were sitting on the bench outside.

"Hi," I croaked.

"You sound horrible," Mr. Martin said.

"Thanks," I said. And I meant it. When you're sick, you want people to notice. Pity feels good in small doses. "Yeah, I sound a lot worse than I feel. I'm actually feeling great. I'll be in tip-top condition for singing on Saturday."

"And the band's goin' good?" Furry asked.

"Couldn't be better," I said.

Just then, Molly appeared around the corner. She walked up to us silently, looked me in the eye . . . and punched me in the stomach. Hard.

I let out a weird, high-pitched gasp that was as embarrassing a sound as I'd ever made. It sounded like a cartoon character heaving. I felt like I might heave. I even felt like a cartoon character.

Molly walked into the barbershop and slammed the door behind her without a word.

"Good thing I got out of the dang music racket when I did," said Furry. "It looks painful."

What was it with the stomach punching? I shrugged at the two men on the bench. They shrugged back.

"Sorry, I know I'm s'posed be older and wiser," said Furry. "But I'm just older. I'm getting un-wiser by the minute."

I opened the door carefully. I thought I might get attacked again. But Molly was sitting in the barber chair, and Edwin wasn't there.

I shrugged my shoulders in a what-the-heck-was-that-for? sort of way.

"Oh, I don't know," Molly said. "Maybe for blowing me off the entire weekend?"

"What? I totally forgot." A lie. Since she had wanted to get together and since I wasn't about to tell her why I didn't want to (a crippling case of Misterfistophobia), I pretended it slipped my mind and poured on the excuses.

"I'm sorry. I went on a camping trip to hell and back with my father. Tons of fun. Near death by monsoon. Nearer death by black flies. My phone didn't get reception. Plus, I got sick. Almost died. Wish you were there."

"A likely story," she said, looking at me hard. "But you do sound sufficiently horrible." She paused for a moment, then gave me a little smile. "Let's see some songs, you tortured genius, you."

Apology apparently accepted.

She flipped through my notebook and couldn't

believe how many I'd written.

"Let's hear this one," she said, pointing to one of the pages.

"Nah," I said. "I'd better save what's left of my voice for the dock." That was true, but I was also suddenly stricken with my old shyness. I guess because I was alone with Molly.

"C'mon, let's hear it. Sing softly."

I took out my guitar and started playing. I just sort of whispered through it.

SONG #8 (first verse):
WHAT A BORE
By Davis Delaware

Get up, get dressed, try not to be depressed
. . . bored.
Sit up, don't be late, listen up and get it
straight . . . bored.
Same thing, every day, each and every stupid
old chore,
What a bore . . . a dull, dumb, stupid old bore.

Molly grabbed my face and kissed me. On the lips.

What the what?

I was confused. First punching, now kissing. And it wasn't exactly a romantic song.

This couldn't be happening. Until now, I didn't know for sure what all the teasing and flirting was about. For a while, I thought she was just kind of messing with me. Now it was definitely starting to seem like she liked me.

And I was sure the Butcher was going to find out and grind me into a paste.

I pushed her away gently—I was sick, after all—but Molly wouldn't stop. She smelled good and looked good and I felt like such an idiot. I mean, this kind of opportunity doesn't come along that often. Like *never*. It occurred to me that getting killed might be a small price to pay for letting her fall into my arms. So I did.

And then the door flew open. "GOTCHA, DWEEB!!" boomed a deep, angry voice.

Oh, god! Mr. Fist! What was I doing?! What was I thinking?!

I shoved Molly away a little too hard, into the counter. "Ow!" she cried.

But it was only Edwin. I didn't know whether to be relieved or pissed. "I wonder what one Gerald 'the Butcher' Boggs would think if he heard about this new development," he said, raising an eyebrow.

"*What* new development?" I asked, sounding as shocked and innocent as possible. I was sweating. "Nothing for him to hear about. We were just messing around." The words kept on coming, even though I hated myself for saying them. "Let's get one thing straight, once and for all. Molly and I are just friends. Period."

Molly's face got red.

"You fools go ahead and practice. I quit," she said, walking out the door.

"But the concert is in two days," Edwin protested. "You *can't* quit."

"Apparently I can," she called, "because I *just did*!"

"Wait a minute!" I said, chasing after her.

"Don't even *think* about following me," she spat, walking quickly down the path. "You're nuts. Maybe I should let Gerald thrash you after all."

There wasn't much I could say to that.

I went back inside the barbershop and looked at Edwin.

"What's going on with her?" I said. "First punching, then kissing . . . now *this*?"

"She and her brother used to punch each other all the time," said Edwin, shrugging. "She punches people she likes. Apparently kisses some of them, too."

I blinked. "But, I mean, she's still with Gerald McMusclehead, right?"

"I think so. Listen, we'd better practice," said Edwin, picking up his bass.

"Yeah, but—did she really quit?"

"Definitely. She's stubborn about stuff like that," said Edwin. "Looks like it's you and me, lover boy. Romeo. Stud muffin."

"Shut up, Edwin."

What the heck? The only reason I even got involved in this was to be in a band with Molly. Now the only

thing I was clear on was that Gerald Neander-creep was more apt to kill me than ever. He had more of a reason to than ever. Molly was probably running to him right now, telling him everything, and sealing my death warrant with a much bigger kiss than the one I got.

I was such an idiot! Just when I found out that Molly actually liked me, I rejected her. No wonder she thought I was nuts. I *was*. It was like when tragic lovers are kept apart by disapproving parents or society or something. Except in this case, *I* was coming between us.

Edwin and I practiced for a while, but my heart wasn't in it and my throat was killing me. We sounded horrible. That was nothing new, but with Molly gone, horrible was all it was.

I tried calling her a bunch of times that night, but she didn't pick up. I left her messages, saying I was sorry, trying to explain, and asking her—fine, I admit it, *begging* her—to come back to the band. No response. She obviously hated me.

Dad had left a note saying that he wasn't getting home until late, and that if I was better, he would pick me up after karate the next day. So I left a note for him, saying that yes, I was feeling good, and yes, that sounded good.

What a joke. I felt anything *but* good, and everything about going to karate sounded unbelievably *bad*. But I couldn't stay home sick again. I had to talk to Molly.

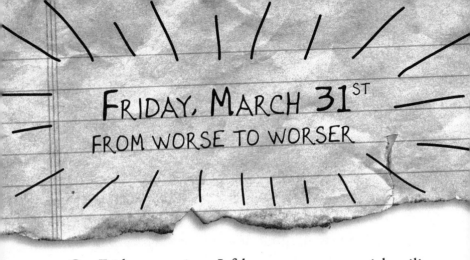

Friday, March 31st
From Worse to Worser

On Friday morning, I felt queasy, woozy, sick, ailing, run-down, and rotten. Pretty much anything in the thesaurus under "horribly, deathly ill." I tried everything—antibiotics, aspirin, cough syrup, that super-numbing throat spray, and lozenge after lozenge—but I still felt like something the cat dragged in . . . after the cat found me lying in the road, having been run over by a car. Make that a truck. An eighteen-wheeler.

But somehow, I made it to school.

My heart was pounding like a sledge-hammer in my head as I walked through the front doors. Every little noise—footsteps, whispers, the sound of my eyes blinking—sounded like a car alarm. My scalp was prickly, hair follicles electrified, brain buzzing. My nose was running, my eyes hurt, my joints ached, and my throat felt like it was on fire. I think my hair *was* on fire.

So, yeah. I didn't feel so good.

And surprise: Molly was absent. There was no point in me even being there. Wonderful.

The Butcher was waiting at my locker after first period. He wore a weirdly dead expression, like he had finally run out of patience. I could tell that he was sick of all the roadblocks preventing him from pulverizing me.

"Hello, dweeb," he said, crossing his arms. "Sensei Jo-Jo says that I should give you a private lesson today. We might need to use the workout room in the back. You know, just so we can get some real learning in."

Real learning. I did not like the sound of that.

"So," Gerald went on, "see you at ka-rah-tay."

But he didn't leave. He just stood there, leaning in close to me and staring while I nervously worked my locker combination.

He just kept repeating, "See . . . you . . . at . . . *ka-rah-tay.*"

My lock finally opened, but the door was jammed again. I yanked as hard as I could, and it unstuck. This time, it slammed the Butcher hard in the knee.

"OW! You pathetic dweeb!" he yelped, holding his knee and balancing on his other leg.

"I didn't mean to do that," I croaked. This was the *second* time I'd accidentally assaulted the Butcher. Good work.

"Yeah, right," he sneered. "Well, then I won't mean what I'm about to do to *you*."

I could only imagine.

Just then, Mr. Rigo walked out of his office. It turned out that my locker was in a convenient location.

"Is there a problem, boys?" he asked, coming toward us.

"No," the Butcher and I said quickly, simultaneously.

"Are you sure?" Rigo asked. "It definitely sounded like a problem." He peered at the "DEAD DWEEB" on my locker door. "What have we here?"

"Wow, I hadn't noticed that, sir," said Gerald.

I wasn't about to rat out the Butcher. "Me neither."

"Kind of hard to miss," said Rigo, rubbing his fingers across the etched skull and letters. "Gerald, I'd like to speak to you in my office. Alone."

"I didn't do it, sir," the Butcher lied. Not very convincingly, either.

Rigo just raised an eyebrow and turned back to me.

"I have no idea," I said, shrugging my shoulders.

Rigo rolled his eyes. "Okay, Mr. Boggs, let's go."

They went off together, and I headed to my next class. Oh, man . . . now I had gotten the Butcher into trouble. Without even meaning to. That's something you definitely do *not* want to do to an alpha goon.

I didn't know exactly what went down in Rigo's office. He didn't have proof of anything, but it was all pretty obvious. I heard the Butcher got detention and that, since spring break was about to start, his parents would come in after to discuss the locker situation.

None of that did anything to slow the Butcher's Campaign of Intimidation. All day long, he kept sneaking up on me in the hallway, grunting like a wildebeest: "See . . . you . . . at . . . *ka-rah-tay.*" The sixth or seventh time, he really got to me. His weird and ominous pronunciation of "ka-rah-tay" was on a permanent loop in my brain. I even heard it when he wasn't around.

I definitely was *not* going to ka-rah-tay. But Dad was picking me up at ka-rah-tay, and I couldn't bring myself to tell him that I wanted to *quit* ka-rah-tay. And I had to go to the dock the next day—as a matter of pride, and because I'd promised Edwin—so I couldn't use the fact that my fevered brain was bubbling like lava as an excuse to *skip* ka-rah-tay . . . ka-rah-tay . . . ka-rah-tay.

When the last bell rang, I went to my locker and grabbed my backpack. I snuck out the back door, across the football field, and into the woods. My head was spinning. I felt like a wimpy little squirrel running for cover. The crunching of leaves under my feet was amplified in my burning ears. I was sweating, and my pulse pounded in my brain. That rhythm was faster than the rhythm of my footsteps. Have you ever heard a drum solo you thought would never end? Well, this was like two drum solos playing simultaneously—both bad, and both way too loud. It was like the whole world was kicking me in the head.

I found a spot under a tree and sat down. I would wait it out. When the time came, I would get over to the Dojo of Death to meet Dad. I'd time it so I would arrive just before everyone got out, so the Butcher wouldn't see me.

How did this happen? How did my promising new start in a new school turn into such an old disaster? Dad was right. I *was* quitting again.

I felt sick. Lovesick and sick-sick. And I was exhausted. Girls, fear, and fever can really wipe a guy out.

I leaned back against the tree and closed my eyes. I felt the pulse in my temples. At least there was only one bad drum solo now. And even that was starting to fade. Having my eyes closed was by far the best feeling I'd had all day.

GIRL IN THE MIST

I hadn't noticed the fog rolling in. It was cooler now. Sunlight filtered through the branches like in a sappy movie, when something super-sappy is about to happen. I heard a twig snap, and there was Molly walking toward me through the trees. She looked more beautiful than ever.

I stood up to greet her.

She gave me a once-over . . . and started to laugh.

I looked down and saw that I wasn't wearing pants.

Lots of other kids popped out from behind trees, and they were laughing and pointing, too.

I screamed.

I turned to run and slammed into a tree.

My eyes eventually opened. It had all been a bad dream. Except the slamming-into-the-tree part—that was real.

I was lying flat on my back. I rubbed my forehead and felt a huge lump. Then I noticed that the sun was going down. I glanced at my watch: 5:26. Dad would be at the dojo any minute.

I leaped to my feet and almost fell down again. I was dizzy. I'd never been delirious before, but this must have been it.

I took off, out of the woods and into the nearby neighborhood. I cut through lawns. I ran as fast as I could, looking around, hoping no  one would see me. A crazed terrier in one yard lunged and sunk his teeth into my pants at the ankle. I yanked hard, tearing the fabric halfway up my leg in the process. I leaped and vaulted over a fence, landed on my back, popped up, and kept running. I felt like I was in a war movie—darting from tree to house to parked car to tree again. I was huffing and puffing and zigzagging like a crazy person.

Maybe I *was* a crazy person.

DOWN AT THE END OF DOJO STREET

I got to the block of the dojo and hid behind a parked truck. I tried to catch my breath. The drums started up in my ears again. The coast was clear. No one on the sidewalk. A few bored parents waited in cars. I made a break for it, ducking around the side of the building.

It would take the class a few minutes to pack up and get out the door, so I'd wait there until I saw  Dad's car, then run out and hop in.

5:33 PM:

Dad wasn't always so good at being on time. I wasn't really sure what direction he'd be coming from, so I kept looking both ways, nervously peeking around the corner, checking the door of the Dojo of Death.

5:37 PM:

I saw Dad's car pull up to a stoplight way down the street.

A few kids started coming out of the dojo. No Butcher. The car was getting closer. No Butcher.

The car arrived. I snuck out onto the sidewalk, trying to mingle with other karate kids. And then, out of the corner of my eye, I saw a huge, unmistakable shape.

Yes, Butcher.

But it was okay. The car was right there, too. I turned toward the Butcher and nodded and waved, making it look to my dad like I'd had a good class and was making friends. The timing could not have been better.

Except that when I reached for the door handle, I realized that Sparky was right next to me, also reaching for the handle. Why was this little twerp trying to get into my car?

Wait a minute. Who was the weird dude with a mustache behind the wheel? And why were the car seats blue, and not black? The obvious answer was that this was the right model, but the wrong car. But my fevered brain wanted to run through all the completely illogical explanations first: Dad had grown a mustache in one day, he'd had the seats reupholstered, he had adopted Sparky to take my place. . . .

"Jerk!" said Sparky, sliding onto the front seat and slamming the door.

"Munchkin!" I replied.

The car sped away.

When I turned around, the Butcher was in my face.

"Gee," he sneered, "too bad that wasn't your daddy-poo. And too bad you missed classy-poo."

I couldn't think of anything to say but, "Yeah, well, next time, I guess."

"But, dweeby-poo," Gerald said with an expression of unbelievably fake concern, "I really feel bad. I mean, you're new and everything. I'd be happy to give you that private lesson right here on the sidewalk."

"No, that's okay . . . I'm actually not feeling that well, anyway. . . ." My mind was racing. What had Molly told him? Did he know about the kiss?

"Lesson one!" the Butcher barked. He leaped up and landed with the loud slap of sneakers on concrete, feet spread and hands in the classic ready-to-kick-your-scrawny-butt position.

"No, really," I said, "next time is fine. I'm looking forward to it."

"MORO ASHI DACHI!"

"Moro *ashi what-chi?*"

"FIGHTING STANCE! MORO ASHI DACHI!"

There were a few kids still waiting for rides, and they all got interested fast.

"Umm . . ." I said, holding my hands up in the classic I'm-an-idiot-who-doesn't-know-what-the-heck-he's-doing position. I mean, my one karate lesson had been given by a glorified toddler.

"MORO ASHI DACHI!" the Butcher cried again. "MORO ASHI DACHI!"

He was saying it in that clipped karate way that, unfortunately, struck me as funny. Must have been the fever. I closed my eyes for a second and laughed to myself.

At least, I thought it was to myself.

"Are you *laughing* at me?" Gerald barked.

My eyes snapped open.

"No, no, not at all." I scrambled to find something to say, but my head wasn't cooperating. "It's just that this is turning into a pretty bad day—"

"Really? That's weird, because it sounded exactly

like you were laughing at me." With that, Gerald started throwing all kinds of kicks and punches. Not hitting me, just terrorizing me . . . and showing off.

"AGE ZUKI! CHOKU ZUKI! HAISHU UKE! EMPI UCHI!"

And just as I was starting to think that this demented demonstration of his would go on forever, he lunged.

"HIRAKEN ZUKI!!!!!"

I stuck my arms out straight, out of instinct, and shoved my stiffened fingers as hard as I could in his direction. My long guitar-picking fingernail stabbed him right in the eye.

"O W W - O O O - O W W - OOOOO!" howled Gerald, holding his face in his hands.

Oh, god.

"Sorry! I didn't mean to do that!" I said.

"OWW-OOO-OWW-OOOOO!"

He sounded like a wounded Sasquatch.

How did this keep happening? This was the *third* time I'd hurt him. It was like waving a red cape at a bull. Except I was actually stabbing the bull in the eye.

Bull's-eye.

The other kids were stunned. A couple of cars pulled up, and Gerald got quiet and turned away from the

173

street. He walked toward the dojo, hiding his face. The cars picked kids up and drove off.

Before long, it was just me and the Butcher. Wonderful.

He was leaning against the wall, holding his eye, breathing heavily. I didn't know what to do. It was completely possible that I had blinded him.

I walked up to him slowly. "Ummm . . . you all right, Gerald?" No answer. "Gerald?"

"DON'T EVER CALL ME THAT!" he seethed. He spun around, and this time he didn't bother with any fancy stances or terminology.

He just slugged me in the eye. Hard.

My head snapped back and the pain shot through my brain, which sounded like it literally rattled around in my skull.

Worst. Drum. Solo. Ever.

I saw a flash of colors and leaned back.

"How do *you* like it?" Gerald yelled.

Somehow, I didn't fall over. I just slowly slumped to the sidewalk. My dad pulled up as I reached a seated position. I looked over at the Butcher.

"An eye for an eye . . ." I mumbled. "I guess we're even."

"No way," he hissed. "We're not even till you're dead. See you at the dock tomorrow."

IN THE CAR

I got into the car and was able to hide my budding black eye from Dad, since it was on my right side.

"Tough practice?" he asked with a smile.

"Not too bad."

"Who was that kid you were with? A new buddy?"

"Yup. New good buddy." Somehow I said that without laughing.

"See? Didn't I tell you karate was a good idea?" Dad sounded proud of himself.

"Yup."

He glanced at me as he pulled out into the street. "You sound terrible. Are you still sick?"

"No, no . . . I feel fine," I croaked pathetically. I wasn't even convincing myself.

"No you don't," he said. "You're going back to bed. For the entire weekend."

It was hard to argue with that. I was sick, tired, scared, and in pain. My entire body hurt—inside and out. Bed sounded good. Really good.

We rode along in silence. That was it. I wasn't going to the dock. I was glad I was sick. It was the perfect excuse. I would call Edwin and explain. Without Molly, the Dweebs sucked, anyway. What was the point?

I watched the houses and buildings go by out the car window. I had actually fooled myself into believing that my life was getting better. I'd just started to not feel like a total misfit. But then everything went bad. Beyond bad.

I would drag myself back to school with my tail between my legs after spring break. Everyone would ask why I hadn't shown up at the dock. But they would know that it was because of the Butcher. The Butcher had won. Butchers always win. I was really sick, but that thought made me feel about a hundred times sicker. Especially since people were actually liking me. They *liked* those poems. They might have liked them even more as *songs*.

If only. The Dweebs—this performance—might have been the best thing I'd ever done.

Then I thought about my mom. I remembered talking to her once when she was sick in bed. I was complaining about wanting to do something, and some jerk at school saying I was a moron. I don't remember which jerk. There had been so many. I was clueless about how sick Mom was at the time, so it didn't seem like what she said was some big piece of advice or anything. I don't know now whether Mom knew she was dying, but I sure didn't. She didn't really seem that sick, anyway, just sort of tired. Heart failure doesn't show on the outside.

Anyway, she said that she'd always wished she'd written a book. She'd had an idea for one and I think she had started writing a few chapters or at least making some notes or something. But then she had me. And a job. And a house and a husband and a million other things. And she was never able to get back to it. She knew that she'd made certain choices, and she didn't regret them. But she had realized something: She'd wimped out. I told her she was wrong, but Mom said no, there had

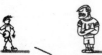

been plenty of time. Just the bad TV alone added up to enough time to write a book. Maybe more than one.

She said that when you really want to do something, there are a million reasons not to do it. There are people who'll say it's stupid and that you're stupid for even thinking about it. There might even be people who go out of their way to get *in* your way.

"You can go ahead and blame those people if you want," Mom said. "It's not their fault if you wimp out."

I thought about how I was riding shotgun in Dad's car, where my mom used to sit. I looked out the window and saw a couple of kids playing catch, and a guy mowing his lawn. It reminded me of the funeral, when I realized that no matter what, the world keeps going.

If I wimped out on Rock Around the Dock, I wouldn't live it down for the rest of the year, or next year, or the year after. It would be my new "Urine Trouble, Pee Boy." No doubt about it, I was scared—it really did seem like the Butcher was capable of just about anything. But as hard as it was to face him, *not* facing him would be worse. Not showing up was quitting, quitting like I'd never quit before. And even though Molly was out—maybe *because* she was out—the show had to go on. I had screwed everything up so badly with her that I couldn't bear to screw this up, too.

"You know, Davis," said Dad, "this has been a tough

time, but I think things are turning around for us."

I looked over at him. He was there to pick me up. He always was. He probably hated his job more than I hated school. I was sure there were tons of things he'd rather be doing than working where he did. His boss was probably a lot like Gerald. I imagined Gerald's dad being my dad's boss. What a nightmare. Dad was trying. Being a terrible cook didn't take any less effort than being a good one. He wasn't the best at understanding me, but I realized that I wasn't the best at understanding him, either. And it was pretty great when we were laughing in that tent.

My dad ↓

← the Butcher's dad

"Hey, Dad," I said. "I'm sorta supposed to play in a band tomorrow . . . you know, a rock band. At the canal."

He glanced over at me, eyebrow raised. "Since when?"

"Since . . . I forgot to tell you." I tried to play it cool. No big deal.

"Well, sorry, but you're still way too sick."

Yeah, this was a mistake.

"No, I feel good. Please, I have to—"

"Forget it."

We rode along in silence again. I wasn't about to bring up my mom's deathbed speech. He didn't need to hear that.

When we got to the house, I went in ahead and said I wasn't hungry for dinner. Dad told me to take my temperature. So I did. But he didn't need to know it was 103. I shook the thermometer down just as he came in.

"See? Normal," I said.

"Still, you're not going anywhere tomorrow. I have to go into the office, and I want you under the covers all day."

"Okay, okay," I said. "Good night, then." I closed my door and got ready for bed.

But once Dad was gone, I called Edwin to make sure he was still in for Rock Around the Dock. Of course he was. I also called Molly . . . and got her voice mail again. But this time, I couldn't even speak. I couldn't think of another way to apologize. I'd left so many messages already. I didn't say anything for what seemed like an eternity, then muttered, "Whatever," and hung up.

Molly wasn't coming—that's all there was to it. But I told myself it really wasn't about Molly or Edwin or the Butcher or the Dweebs anymore. It was about me. I would not wimp out.

I needed to get to the dock by eleven thirty the next morning, so I set my alarm for ten, just to be safe.

Then I quietly went over songs in my head until I passed out.

SATURDAY, APRIL 1ST
FISTFUL OF COUGH DROPS

BAAAAAAAAAA! My alarm sounded like a sheep with an upstate New York accent. It felt like I had just fallen asleep. My throat was sore, and I was incredibly tired. I hit the snooze button.

I guess I must have hit it a bunch more times, because when I finally woke up, it was 11:10.

I leaped to my feet. My head was throbbing. I looked in the mirror. The whole right side of my face—from my forehead to my cheek—was black and blue and greenish. Thanks, Gerald. Thanks,

Thanks, tree.

tree. I thought about maybe going into my dad's room and looking through my mom's old stuff to see if there was some kind of makeup to cover it up. But I couldn't

bring myself to do that. It probably wouldn't have worked, anyway. I mean, if Gerald noticed it, he'd just have one more reason to kill me. I took some aspirin instead.

I had to hurry. What to wear? I should have thought this through. I didn't have anything in my closet or my drawers that looked vaguely rock-star-esque. That was okay, I guessed. The Amazing Dweebs should really look as dweeby as possible. It was just that, somehow, I was hoping for dweeby-cool as opposed to dweeby-dweeby.

I sifted through the clothes on the floor and under the bed . . . and then I saw it. Molly's Mad Manny the Monkey shirt. I'd totally forgotten that I had it.

I tried it on. Molly was right. It was tight— rock-band tight. The shirt would definitely make the Butcher that much more rabid. But at the moment, I didn't care. I might as well look cool while getting killed. He wasn't really going to *murder* me in front of all those people, was he? And like Molly said, it was the perfect shirt for the leader of a band called the Amazing Dweebs.

Dad had left me a note in the kitchen: "Please eat something for breakfast . . ." Too late. I had to get out of there. ". . . and then go right back to bed!" Okay, *that* wasn't gonna happen.

I spotted Dad's sunglasses on the counter and put them on to cover up my black eye. They didn't do much to hide the entire black, blue, and green side of my face, or the gigantic lump on my forehead. Oh, well. I told myself that I looked hard core, put my guitar in its case, grabbed a fistful of cough drops, and headed out.

It wasn't that long of a walk to the canal and the dock. I'd make it there in about fifteen minutes. I sucked furiously on a cough drop, nervously crunched it to bits, then popped in another one. I walked as fast as I could. I tried to sing a little, but it wasn't until then that I realized I hardly had a voice at all. My throat didn't hurt as much as before, but I sounded like a frog with a frog in his throat.

A FROG
WITH A FROG
IN HIS THROAT

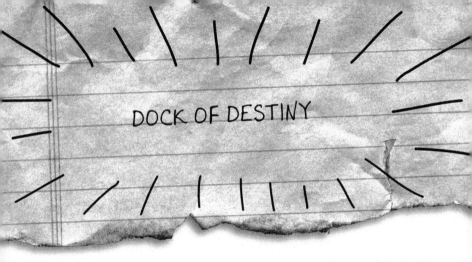

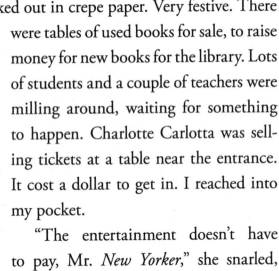

When I got to the dock, it was already crowded. The barge was decked out in crepe paper. Very festive. There were tables of used books for sale, to raise money for new books for the library. Lots of students and a couple of teachers were milling around, waiting for something to happen. Charlotte Carlotta was selling tickets at a table near the entrance. It cost a dollar to get in. I reached into my pocket.

"The entertainment doesn't have to pay, Mr. *New Yorker*," she snarled, sounding weirdly annoyed as she waved me in. I figured she was bored having to sit there with the cash box. Maybe something else about the event was bothering her poetic sensibilities.

"Thanks," I said, moving into the

crowd. Danderbrook wiggled her fingers at me from behind one of the book tables.

Everyone was talking, but then suddenly it got a lot quieter—just a few hushed whispers. It's like when you think everybody's been talking about you. Usually, that's not true. But in this case, it definitely was.

Ivan Brink, the chubby vampire, was standing with Sparky, the kid from the dojo. I realized then that they looked a lot alike. Sparky was Ivan's little brother. Of course.

Ivan pointed and shouted to me, "Look out! The Butcher's right behind you!"

I almost had a heart attack.

"April Fool's!" he said, laughing. Sparky laughed even louder.

"Very funny, you two." I had forgotten it was April Fool's Day.

"Sorry, Dela-who," Ivan said. He didn't sound all that sorry. "Hey, cool shades. Cool shiner, too. Heard you gouged out a big chunk of the Butcher's eye."

"Yeah," said Sparky, smiling, "and his dad's a lawyer. They're probably gonna sue the crap outta your mom and dad." He really didn't like me.

"Oh, my mom and dad, huh?" I whispered, accidentally sounding a bit like Clint Eastwood. Maybe the laryngitis was working for me. "Well, my mom's dead," I continued coldly, thinking that would shut him up. It didn't.

"April Fool's?" asked Sparky.

"No, Sparky," I whispered threateningly.

"Idiot," said Ivan, rolling his eyes. "His mom *is* dead. Everybody knows that." Then he turned to me. "But still, Dela-who, it's illegal in martial arts to grow your fingernails into long sabers and stab them in the other guy's eyes and stuff. I mean, it's cool, but illegal."

"It's totally illegal," Sparky echoed, but in a snotty tone.

"My fingernail is for playing the guitar," I said, strumming the air. "Plus, it was self-defense."

"So, what's in there?" asked Sparky, poking at my guitar case with his index finger.

What kind of weird question was that? What was with this kid?

"What do you think?" I asked. "Guitar, notebooks, lyrics . . ."

"Yeah, idiot," said Ivan, "what do you think?"

Edwin arrived then, and blew right by me.

"Edwin!" I croaked.

"Hurry up, Delaware!" he barked impatiently. "What the heck happened to your voice?"

What was his problem?

He had a point, though. We were up first, so we had to get going.

I ran to catch up with him. "It's called laryngitis."

"It's called a nightmare," Edwin said, glancing over at me. "Speaking of which, what happened to your *face?* I thought you were sleeping like a baby, safely in your bed."

"Hard mattress," I said.

Mr. Shettle was guarding the gangplank like a bouncer. Gym teachers make good bouncers.

"Where do you think you're going, Delaware?" Shettle barked.

"Croaky's with me," said Edwin. "We're the entertainment."

"Oh, right . . . entertainment," said Shettle, shaking his head and rolling his eyes. "Go ahead, Eddie. I guess Black-and-Blue Boy can go, too."

"Thanks, Uncle Larry," said Edwin.

Eddie? Uncle Larry? Rewind, please.

"Shettle is your *uncle*?" I said, following Edwin across the gangplank and onto the barge. "April Fool's?"

Edwin wasn't laughing. "Nope. He's my mother's brother."

I guess that explained why Shettle didn't seem to care when Edwin strolled in so late to gym class.

I grabbed his arm. "I can't believe you never mentioned that!"

"You never asked," he said, yanking his arm away.

Why on Earth would I possibly think to ask him that?

"So, Molly's not going to show," I said, trying to sound like I didn't care.

"Forget her," Edwin said. "She's way too cool to be hanging around with a couple of dweebs like us. Why are you wearing that crappy shirt, anyway? It looks ridiculous."

What was *with* him today? I didn't answer.

The deck of the barge was covered with cables. Some student-council kids were working as tech support, setting up and plugging things in.

"I need to find a bathroom," I said.

Edwin and I put down our guitars and headed toward the back of the barge. Edwin used the tiny, stinky bathroom first, and I called to him through the door.

"What's wrong? I mean, it seems like something is bothering you."

"Nope," said Edwin flatly.

Okay, I admit, I hadn't known the guy that long. But when Edwin Martin gives a one-word answer to any question, something is definitely wrong.

SHOWTIME

Back on the stage, I took out my guitar. My notebooks weren't in the case. I must have left them at home, in my rush to get out of the house. But I could have sworn I'd brought them.

Wonderful.

Everything was so screwed up. No lyrics, no voice, no Molly, weirder-than-usual Edwin. But the show would go on, because it *had* to go on. Without the show, I had nothing. This was my chance to prove myself to the whole school. I remembered the words to some of the songs, so since I didn't have my notebooks for reference, those would just have to be the songs I'd sing.

I looked down into the crowd and spotted the Butcher. He was wearing a black eye patch, which made him look like a tough, crazy-angry pirate. Ominous. He and all his goons were right up in front, peering up at the stage with smiles on their faces. The kind of smiles that say, *We are sooo happy to be here . . . and sooo happy to see you* fail.

The rest of the audience was ready to hear something, anything. Someone hollered that they wanted to hear the Amazing Dweebs play.

"Hey, where's Molly?" yelled someone else.

"Yeah," said Willard Gourdinski, vibrating with anger. "Without her, you're just plain old dweebs. Nothing *amazing* about it."

Gourdinski was right. We were nothing without Molly.

Edwin picked up his bass and plugged it in. We set up about six feet apart, but he barely looked at me. He was completely stone-faced. I plugged in my guitar and turned on the amp, which crackled and hummed. That got some applause.

Edwin was screwing around with the bass, plucking a few random notes, pretending to know what he was doing even though he obviously didn't. When it came right down to it, we had barely practiced at all, so Edwin hadn't gotten much better. I started tuning and tried hard to look cool, like I wasn't a swollen purple-faced loser on a dirty barge on a smelly canal.

After a minute, I noticed a pretty girl I'd never seen before staring at me from the crowd. I mean *pretty*. She

waved to me. Just one wave, her arm bent at the elbow like a slow-motion windshield wiper. It seemed like she was saying, *I see you . . . do you see me? We know each other.*

Or maybe I was just delusional.

I squinted and stared, but I had absolutely no idea who the girl was. She pointed her finger at her head and drew circles in the air — the universal symbol for *You are out of your freaking mind, you crazy black-and-blue lunatic.* So I guess she didn't know me. She just knew exactly what she thought of me.

Danderbrook walked over and leaned into the microphone. "I trust Mr. Delaware has finally tuned that guitar."

Everyone laughed.

"What on Earth happened to your face?" she asked me, covering the mic.

"You don't want to know," I mumbled.

"Okay, then," she said, turning back to the microphone. "Hi, everybody! Thanks for coming down to Rock Around the Dock! This year, we have two great bands here to raise a little money for a good cause: the school library!"

The smattering of applause was nearly drowned out by widespread groaning.

Danderbrook continued: "Okay, okay, let's get started! First up, the new band on the bill. This is fitting for a library benefit, since the band's leader is a new student who has made quite a mark in the English department at Woodrow Wilson in a very short period of time. Without further ado, here are the Amazing Dweebs!" She gestured to me and Edwin, then headed for the gangplank to join the crowd.

The crowd cheered, clapped, hooted, hollered, booed, and laughed. All at once.

"All right," I croaked into the microphone, which squealed with feedback. "Hello, Rock Around the Dock." I felt totally embarrassed saying that. It was like ordering a Rooty Tooty Fresh 'N Fruity. Having to say it almost makes you not want it.

But when I looked out at the crowd, I knew that I *did* want it. I wanted to be there. I wanted to perform. I was tired of being scared of the Butcher, and there was nothing he could say or do to stop me. Maybe it was the fever, but I just didn't care about him anymore. I didn't care that Edwin seemed to be cranky or grumpy or whatever. I didn't care that I sounded like a froggy Clint Eastwood. If your voice is reduced to a whisper, sounding like any kind of Clint Eastwood is probably the way to go.

I didn't even care that Molly hadn't shown up.

Me as Clint Eastwood

But then she did show up. And I realized that I did care. A lot.

There was a commotion in the crowd as she worked her way toward the barge. She crossed the gangplank and walked right up to me. The Butcher watched her like a hawk.

She was wearing my sweatshirt. She looked beautiful.

She moved in close to the microphone. "Nice shirt," she said.

"You, too."

Molly punched me gently in the stomach, holding her fist against me for a second, and whispered, "It was that last message. Especially the super-long pause—I mean

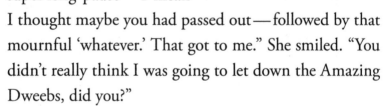

I thought maybe you had passed out—followed by that mournful 'whatever.' That got to me." She smiled. "You didn't really think I was going to let down the Amazing Dweebs, did you?"

I didn't know *what* to think. Was Molly there because she liked me despite everything, and finally knew how much I liked her? After all this time, I still hadn't revealed that. In fact, I'd denied it. Repeatedly. At this point, Molly would have to have been a mind reader to have a clue what I thought about her. Maybe she still hated me and was only there for the Dweebs.

I couldn't know, but it didn't matter. She was there.

Molly looked over at Edwin, and he smiled. She had this ability to make people feel good, even when two seconds earlier, they were feeling horrible or pissed off or whatever Edwin was feeling.

"We've barely practiced at all," I said quietly.

Molly thought for a second. "How about the song you sang when I kissed you? I remember that one. I'll sing harmony again."

"Yes," I said.

Hell yes, I thought. *She* brought up that moment. That had to be a good thing.

I felt prouder than I'd ever felt. I was standing onstage with Molly. We'd be singing a song I wrote, sharing a microphone in front of everyone. We were sharing each others' shirts, too, and everyone knew that meant something. For the first time, I allowed myself to think that maybe we could be together.

I noticed that other girl in the crowd again. Then I saw Molly noticing her. "Come on, Delaware," she said, snapping in front of my face. "We haven't got all day."

I looked over at Edwin. "It's just E, A, and B7. Keep the bass line simple."

SONG #8 (full version):
WHAT A BORE
By Davis Delaware

Get up, get dressed, try not to be
  depressed . . . bored.
Sit up, don't be late, listen up and get it
  straight . . . bored.

Same thing, every day, each and every stupid
  old chore,
What a bore . . . a dull, dumb, stupid old bore.

Same thing everywhere, every kid in every
  chair . . . bored.
In class, down the hall, starting every single
  Fall . . . bored.
Same thing, every day, each and every stupid
  old chore,
What a bore . . . a dull, dumb, stupid old bore.

On the chorus, I held up my hand to let people in the crowd know that they should sing, too. It's not like there were a lot of words to learn:

We're bored, bored, bored, bored, bored, bored, bored, bored, bored,
Bored, bored, bored, bored, bored, bored, bored, bored, bored,
Bored, bored, bored, bored, bored, bored, bored, bored, bored,
What a bore . . . a dull, dumb, stupid old bore.

It was funny to hear a crowd of people screaming the word "bored" that many times. Any word loses its meaning when you repeat it a lot. After the first line of "boreds," it sounded like a bunch of aliens or an idling motorboat or something.

There were two more verses:

Don't talk, take a test, welcome to the cuckoo's nest . . . bored.
Memorize, anesthetize, gotcha right between the eyes . . . bored,
Same thing, every day, each and every stupid old chore,

What a bore . . . a dull, dumb, stupid old bore.

*Day in, day out, lose your mind without a doubt . . .
bored.*
Work hard, get a job, turn into a big blob . . . bored.
*Same thing, every day, each and every stupid old
chore,*
What a bore . . . a dull, dumb, stupid old bore.

*Same thing, every day, each and every stupid old
chore,*
What a bore . . . a dull, dumb, stupid old bore.

The crowd went wild. I mean, they always say that, but this crowd really seemed wild.

Unbelievably, the Dweebs actually sounded okay. Edwin's bass was better than expected. Molly's harmony wasn't perfect, but it felt perfect. My "froggy Eastwood" had sort of morphed into "old blues singer East-wood," and it sounded like I was there to tell them what was what. Like I was Dirty Howlin' Wolf Harry, who had rambled up from the delta, down a thousand lonesome highways, and knew a little something about boredom and life in general—and, yes, I felt lucky about it, punk.

The song summed up how bored I'd felt for most of my life, but I was feeling anything but bored now. I was smiling. Molly was smiling.

The Butcher was not smiling.

A SONG TOO FAR

A few kids from Danderbrook's class started chanting for the song version of that other poem I'd recited for them, "Full of Bleep." I'd never even tried singing it.

"Full of Bleep! Full of Bleep!" they cried.

Molly leaned over. "I think you'd better do that 'Full of Bleep' thing before a bleeping riot breaks out."

"Good bleeping idea," I said, grinning.

I started playing. Coming up with chords for any song is pretty easy when you only know a few chords to begin with. I started in quietly, beating out a rhythm. Edwin joined in, and I nodded. Simple.

SONG #9:
FULL OF BLEEP
By Davis Delaware

Hey, you, you're such a jerk!
Yeah, you, you're such a creep!
Hey, you, your head don't work!
Yeah, you, you're full of bleep!

Hey, you, your face is red!
Yeah, you, you're such a creep!
Hey, you, you wet your bed!
Yeah, you, you're full of bleep!

After that second verse, a small group of classmates started singing along and laughing. They were really cracking up. A couple were almost choking from laughter.

Huh?

I thought the song was kind of funny, but I didn't quite get their reaction.

Hey, you, you are so stupid!

201

Yeah, you, you're such a creep!
What's that smell, I think you poop-ed!
Yeah, you, you're full of bleep!

Speaking of stupid, that was a really stupid rhyme. But it seemed to be very effective at bringing Gerald's blood to a boil. He had moved from merely full of rage to seriously demented. Even Molly stopped singing and looked back and forth nervously between the Butcher and me.

Shettle was still guarding the plank. I was actually happy to see him there. So even though it looked like the Butcher's head was about to explode, it was okay by me. There were city workers around to clean that stuff up.

A large part of the audience was now chanting, "Yeah, you, you're full of bleep!" Then I noticed that the kids who were laughing the hardest were pointing at Gerald in rhythm with the song.

Edwin inched toward me. He leaned in and spoke loudly over the racket. "You know why they're laughing?"

I shrugged and kept slamming out the chords.

Edwin chuckled. "Get this: Gerald was a bed wetter all through elementary school."

What?!

Good god. I had no idea.

"And," Edwin hollered over the noise of the crowd,

"nothing drives him more insane than someone making fun of him for it. In sixth grade, Paul Kamurski was joking around about it behind Gerald's back, not realizing that he was *literally* behind Gerald's back. Kamurski left on a stretcher. Some said he died, and others said he just changed schools. But nobody ever saw him again."

Okay, that was it. I stopped playing.

But Edwin happily joined in the chanting again: "Yeah, you! You're full of bleep!"

OKAY, YOU MAY STOP NOW.
PLEASE. I MEAN IT. NOW.
PRETTY PLEASE?

It seemed like Edwin was intentionally trying to make Gerald blow his top. In fact, Edwin looked like he was beyond excited about it.

"Edwin, *enough*!" I cried, waving, trying to shut the thing down. Molly was frantically making the "cut it" sign with her hand to her throat, too, but stopping the flow of words from Edwin's mouth was like stopping Niagara Falls. He kept smiling and singing and slamming on the bass.

The crowd was totally into it. Even Danderbrook was bopping to the beat, doing some kind of crazy dance from thirty years ago.

Wait a minute . . . where was Gerald? I'd lost track of him in the sea of "Full of Bleep" chanters. I scanned back and forth across the crowd, until I finally saw him. He was . . . reading a book.

So, what? He'd gone shopping at the used-book tables and was suddenly engrossed in his new purchase? This seemed like an extremely odd time for recreational reading. In the middle of a concert? In the middle of revving up to tear me limb from limb? Had he scored a manual on preferred methods of eradicating one's enemies?

Gerald's face was beet red. He looked down at the book, then back up at me. Again and again.

Wait.

NO!

He wasn't reading a regular book. Gerald had *one of my notebooks*. He and the goons were looking through *all* of my notebooks. Somebody had stolen them from my guitar case, I guess while I was in the bathroom.

Who besides the Dweebs even knew they were in there? I racked my brain. Wait a minute.

Sparky.

I scanned the audience and there he was, dead center, looking up at me with a smile that seemed impossibly big

for his tiny face. Why did I have to call him a munchkin?

Everyone else was still chanting, "Yeah, you . . . you're full of bleep!"

Butcher and company riffled through the notebook pages, making wild motions with their hands. Their faces twisted into angry gargoyle expressions. All those horrible portraits and nasty songs! Willard Gourdinski's bees were swarming. I swear I could hear them buzzing. He started ripping out pages and throwing them into the air like confetti.

I didn't know what to do. I was kind of trapped there on the barge, frozen, watching it all unfold. Molly and I watched helplessly as Edwin and the crowd chanted louder and louder, making the Butcher angrier and angrier.

Gerald moved closer to the gangplank, trying to get past Mr. Shettle. But even though Shettle hated me, he was protective of Edwin. Shettle folded his arms and glared at the Butcher. The Butcher gestured and pointed, but Shettle wasn't budging.

"Yeah, you, you're full of bleep! Yeah, you, you're full of bleep!"

Gerald stopped trying to get past Shettle. Instead, he crossed his arms, bit his lip, and closed his eyes. He stood verrrrry still.

Then Gerald—the creep whose entire mission in

life was to make others cry—*started to cry.*

At first, I didn't believe it. But then he looked down and covered his face with his hands. His shoulders heaved. He sobbed.

Pretty soon, everyone noticed. The goons went into catatonic shock. For them, it was like seeing Superman bawl like a baby. One by one, the chanters faded out.

Edwin continued plucking the bass a bit, but eventually even he stopped.

It was dead quiet, except for the sound of the Butcher whimpering. I thought for sure someone would call him crybaby Butcher, or crybaby Gerald, or crybaby *something.* But you could see from the looks on everyone's faces that they actually felt sorry for the brute who had tormented most of them for years.

I felt sorry for him, too.

I remembered Mrs. Toople saying that Gerald and I had a lot in common. She had seemed nuts. Actually, she was nuts. But maybe there was some truth to it. It's like when you realize that King Kong has real emotions and is in love with Fay Wray. He doesn't seem like as much of a monster. He seems less like a cliché . . . and more like you.

A HELPING HAND

Anton Squilt (*n.*: an idiot turd-faced jerk worshipper) held his arms out as if he actually wanted to give the Butcher a hug.

"Hey, buddy," he said, "don't feel so bad." For the first time in Squilt's life, everyone hung on his every word. "We all know you used to wet your bed once in a while," he continued timidly. "Well, more than once in a while."

Oh, man, where was he going with this?

"But that's all water under the bridge . . . oh, I mean . . . you know what I mean. We still like you. So . . . please stop crying, Gerald."

Did he say *Gerald*?

There were a few nervous gasps.

Molly walked up behind me and whispered, "Fasten your seat belts."

Squilt realized his mistake and scrambled to fix it. "I mean Big G . . . G-Man . . . Butcher . . ."

The Butcher's shoulders stopped heaving. His head turned slowly, face pinched and angry. His hurt feelings seemed to turn back into regular old psycho bully feelings right before our eyes.

"LISTEN, YOU MORON," he growled. "I WASN'T *CRYING*, I WAS *KIDDING*!"

Anton Squilt's lip trembled. "Please don't hit me. Please don't hit me. Please don't hit me." Then he stopped, dropped, and rolled into a fetal position. It sounds a little dramatic, but with the Butcher's roar still echoing in the air, it seemed like the sensible thing to do.

The Butcher turned back to Shettle and pointed to something in the notebook. Shettle squinted at the page. Then he read out loud, making every line into a question, like he couldn't believe what he was reading:

"Hey, you, in the gymnasium?
Yeah, you, you're such a creep!"

He stopped for a second to glare at me before continuing:

"Hey, you, so dumb and lazy-um?
Yeah, you, you're full of bleep!"

Now *his* face got red. He and the Butcher looked like two huge angry tomatoes. I would have laughed, if I wasn't afraid for my life.

2 MR. TOMATO HEADS

The Butcher handed Shettle another notebook and pointed out another passage.

Shettle read some more:

"If your head is made of lumber,
You are smarter . . . Shettle's dumb-ber."

That did it. Shettle stepped aside and made a right-this-way-sir kind of motion with his hand, inviting the Butcher aboard the barge. It was like unleashing a mad dog.

Gerald crossed the gangplank in one leap.

I backed away. "Listen, Butcher, I didn't *mean* any of it." No, wait, he'd never believe that. "Actually, I guess I meant some of it. But definitely not the whole bed-wetting thing. I mean, I had no idea you actually had a problem with that."

"Shut up!" he snarled, fake-lunging at me.

This was a variation on the hair-smooth move, and

it worked perfectly. I jerked backward, tripped over an amplifier, and fell hard, flat on my back. I put my hands up, shielding my face.

Gerald bent down toward me, jutting his chin like he was going to chin me to death. "Brainless dweeb. You think you can show up here, and all of a sudden everybody's gonna love you and hate me?"

"No, I—" I realized he was right. It had somehow become a competition for him. Maybe for me, too. Not just for Molly, but for the hearts and minds of the entire school.

But Gerald didn't want to hear it. "SHUT! UP!"

The other goons came up behind him, snickering.

I was so cornered.

"You are so cornered," said Anton Squilt.

"Leave him alone!" screamed Molly, trying to push her way through the crowd of goons surrounding me.

But I knew there was no way they would leave me alone.

"Okay, boys," I heard Danderbrook say. "Break it up."

But before they could even think about breaking it up, someone else shrieked, "WAIT!"

ALL YOU DON'T NEED IS LOVE

It was Ivan Brink. He was waving a page that had been ripped from a notebook. "Listen to this love poem that Dela-who wrote to Molly!"

"What?" said the Butcher, Molly, and Edwin — and a lot of other people — simultaneously.

Please. Lord. No. How much worse could this get? *Which* love poem? There were so many.

"Check this!" said Ivan, beside himself with excitement. "It's called 'Keep It Secret.'"

"No need to read that," I said, sitting up. "No one would find it interesting."

"I'm pretty sure I'd find it interesting," said Molly, crossing her arms.

Ivan cleared his throat. His weird little vampire voice made everything even worse.

SONG #10:
KEEP IT SECRET
By Davis Delaware

See her walking down the street,
Molly always in my head,
Though I worship at her feet,
Keep it secret or I'm dead.

Keep it secret, never tell,
Keep the feelings all unsaid,
Wimpy turtle in his shell,
Keep it secret or I'm dead.

Keep it secret . . . or I'm dead.
Keep it secret . . . or I'm dead.

In retrospect, I have no idea why I repeated that line so many times.

Keep it secret . . . or I'm dead.

Hearing it out loud like that made me want to *be* dead. Each repetition was another nail in my coffin.

Keep it secret . . . or I'm dead.

So that was how Molly finally found out that I actually did like her. A lot. That I had all along. But that I'd pretended not to because I was plain old scared. Wimpy turtle in his shell.

I didn't want to look at her, but I did. Everyone did.

MOLLY SPEAKS

Molly nodded in silence for a moment. She brought the microphone close to her lips. Then she extended her other arm in my general direction, drawing smaller and smaller circles in the air with her index finger, before finally pointing to me.

"Ladies and gentlemen . . . the one, the only, Davis Delaware. The wussiest wuss in the history of wusses." She looked at me for a minute. "And he kisses like a fish."

A *fish*?

Things quickly went from bad to worse.

"Check *this* out!" squealed Willard Gourdinski, twitching like an over-caffeinated poodle. He pointed to something else in a notebook. He had found the Glossary of Goons.

"EWWWW!" whined Karl Kidder, looking over Willard's shoulder and drooling furiously.

"What is it?" Anton Squilt desperately wanted to know.

Other students and teachers passed around different notebooks, recognizing grotesque depictions of themselves.

I heard the lonesome wail of Stephen Jablowski, who had apparently found the entry defining him as a sickly coyote, accompanied by a drawing of him as—you guessed it—a sickly coyote. I remembered having a lot of fun drawing tons of fleas and ticks hopping around on his head.

"WAIT A MINUTE!" A voice cut through the air. Danderbrook.

Finally, the voice of reason.

"*This* is supposed to be *me*?" she cried, pointing in horror to the portrait I had done of her in that first class, days before I'd submitted my poem and become her poetic pet. Good god. I'd spent about twenty minutes carefully rendering slugs slithering in and out of her nostrils.

"WHY?" she wailed. The prince of poetry had let her down. I thought about trying to explain. Maybe say, that, you know, those slugs were just metaphors for something, um, *nice?*

Meanwhile, until Molly said what she said—you know, the thing about me kissing like a fish—the

Butcher probably only suspected that she and I had kissed. Now he knew for sure, and he clearly didn't care that Molly hated me. His hate for me was all that mattered.

The Butcher towered over me like Godzilla. I tried to crawl away, but he grabbed me by the collar and belt and lifted me like a helpless infant. I crawled in midair for a second.

"Have fun swimming with the sharks, dweeb," he said. He started turning, holding me at arm's length. Around and around I flew, like I was on an out-of-control kiddie airplane ride.

The Butcher was enjoying himself way too much. "Three, two, one, zero . . . we . . . have . . . liftoff!"

"STOP!!!!!" someone screamed.

"What? No, *liftoff*! We have *liftoff*!" roared the Butcher, letting me go.

Of course, he meant to throw me overboard, but the *STOP* screwed up his aim and I flew into the drum kit instead, crashing and clanging with the cymbals across the deck.

The scream had to have come from Molly, right? She was coming to my defense after all.

Wrong.

It was Edwin. He clutched the microphone to his chest, until he realized that everyone could hear his heart pounding. Then he lifted it to his mouth.

"There's no point in killing Delaware," he said, turning to me. "First of all, I should probably tell you that I'm the one who scratched 'Dead Dweeb' on your locker."

What?

"I told you I didn't do it," snapped the Butcher, crossing his arms.

"But Edwin," I asked, struggling to my feet. "Why would you do that?"

"Fair question," he said, "and that brings up my second point." He cleared his throat. Then a tidal wave of words gushed out. "I've loved Molly for a lot longer than either of you. She's been trying to break up with the Butcher since last summer. Then you came along,

Davis, with your whole new-guy mystique. And your so-called brilliant poems. They're not even that good, you know. I could write better ones in my sleep. Anyway, I just wanted to scare you."

Dead silence.

Molly and the Butcher looked as shocked as I felt.

"Molly and I were born one day apart, in the same hospital," Edwin continued. "My mom says we cooed and gurgled at each other, making a very deep baby connection."

Wait a minute. *Deep baby connection? New-guy mystique?*

I waited for "April Fool's," but none came. Edwin was serious.

"All those years, Molly never knew," he said, still looking at me. "She didn't know that I saved every single thing she gave me. Anything she touched. Old birthday cards. Those candy hearts with the sayings on them. The bandage from that time she banged her knee on the volleyball court. Remember, Molly? Sixth-grade girls' intramural championships?"

Good god, this was getting a little creepy. And once again, it seemed like Edwin would never stop talking.

"Old book reports, used lollipop sticks, her retainer.

I have a piece of Juicy Fruit she chewed last year in my pocket right now."

"Ewww," everyone said, all at once.

Except for Ivan Brink, who said, "Cool."

Molly was stunned.

We all stood like statues. Edwin had clearly established himself as a major Molly freak.

The Butcher breathed heavily and snorted like a bull. I saw where this was going and it was not going to be pretty. He grunted a couple of times, put his head down, and charged at Edwin. His hands were in the I'm-going-to-strangle-you position that I was so familiar with.

Edwin screamed like a little girl. Molly screamed like a regular-sized girl.

I had to do something.

I tore off after the Butcher and leaped onto his back, wrapping my arms around his thick neck. I thought he'd fall over, but he didn't. I was just a minor inconvenience as he barreled toward Edwin.

Then I did what anyone would do in that situation. Especially anyone who recently enrolled in karate, but, you know, hadn't learned diddly yet. I held on tight with one arm still hooked around his neck, and karate chopped him in the nose with the other.

"KA-POW!" I yelled.

"ARRRRRGGGGHHHH!" screamed Gerald. He elbowed my ribs and twisted and bucked, trying to throw me off. My legs slammed into one of the goons.

"WATCH IT!" Karl Kidder cried and slurped. (*n.*: 3. the Niagara Falls of droolers.)

I karate-chopped the Butcher anywhere I could reach. I yelled out to him in rhythm with the chops: "Don't! You! Ever! Get! Tired! Of! Being! Such! A! Cliché!?"

"SHUT UP!" he howled, followed by, "OUCH! OUCH! OUCH!" He whipped me around in the other direction. This time, my foot popped Willard Gourdinski in the jaw.

"OWWW!"

"Butcher," I hollered. "Remember your karate ethics. You're not exactly 'honoring the principles of etiquette,' here!"

"SHUT! UP!" he cried.

Finally, like a bronco being worn down by a champion buckaroo, the Butcher staggered . . . and went down. Hard. My landing was slightly softer. I landed on him.

We found ourselves at Molly's feet. We both looked up and tried to catch her eye, but she was looking *past* us, like we weren't even there.

"Eddie," she said, "I never knew you cared."

I couldn't believe my ears.

Edwin looked the most surprised of all.

"Hey, wait a minute!" I said. "What about how he *also* never told you he loved you? Only for him, it went on for *your entire life.*"

"Yeah," said Molly, slowly moving toward Edwin, "but we did make that deep baby connection. Plus, he's the smartest kid in school. I do wish he'd returned that retainer, though. I sifted through an entire dumpster looking for that thing."

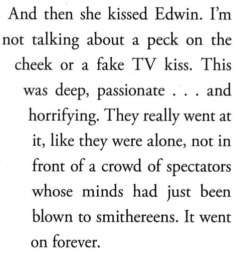

And then she kissed Edwin. I'm not talking about a peck on the cheek or a fake TV kiss. This was deep, passionate . . . and horrifying. They really went at it, like they were alone, not in front of a crowd of spectators whose minds had just been blown to smithereens. It went on forever.

I helped Gerald to his feet. Maybe we could bond over our mutual pain. After all, not only were we both Molly rejects, we also both had humiliating urine-leakage incidents in our past. Who knew?

He peered down at me. "What do you say, Delaware? Let's let bygones be bygones."

"Really?" I said, holding my hand out to shake. I couldn't believe it. Maybe he really wasn't so bad.

Gerald grinned and whispered, "April Fool's." His Clint Eastwood was better than mine.

He poked me hard in the chest with one finger. That was all it took.

I flapped my arms a bit—the way cartoon characters do when they're trying to catch their balance—and fell into the canal.

DOWN UNDER

I hit the cold water hard and sank like a stone, in an explosion of bubbles. But I wasn't scared. In a weird way, it was good just to be off that barge. No more being threatened or laughed at or hated or rejected. A little alone time.

I almost didn't want to come up.

Then I remembered—*your private parts fall off, you slowly bleed to death*—and I panicked. I kicked and thrashed my way to the surface. I swallowed about a gallon of canal scum along the way.

But of course, I didn't die. And of course, there were no sharks down there. The sharks were on the barge and the dock.

BACK ON DRY LAND

I doggy-paddled to the dock ladder and dragged myself up the first rung. Willard Gourdinski, who had apparently raced across the gangplank to greet me, leaned over the edge, vibrated for a moment, and spit. He got me right in my black eye.

That's when I realized that Dad's sunglasses were at the bottom of the canal.

But I kept climbing. Mr. Shettle grabbed my hand and pulled me up the rest of the way. I flopped onto the dock like a flounder. Everyone in the crowd shook their heads and sneered as I picked myself up and sloshed among them, hocking toxic canal loogies.

Charlotte Carlotta, the snobby poetry girl, was standing there with her arms crossed, rolling her eyes at me. "I looked through every single *New Yorker* for the past three years, and you're nowhere to be found, liar. And that was *not* the state song of Delaware!"

A group of cheerleader types—the same ones who,

only days before, were desperate to know me—looked at me like I had cooties, which I probably did (if not something much worse).

"Why don't you just go back to Delaware, where you belong?" said the alpha cheerleader.

Ivan Brink appeared at my side. "That was cool," he said. "Did your private parts fall off?"

I felt nauseous. The weight of the water in my clothes felt like the weight of the entire world.

Danderbook walked up to me, looking concerned. "Are you all right?" she asked.

"Never better," I said, hacking and clearing my throat of flotsam and jetsam, like a seriously ancient mariner.

Then the mystery girl from the crowd approached. What now?

"Hi, Davis Delaware," she said. "You don't remember me, do you?"

"Umm, no . . ." *Spit, hack, blechh.* ". . . actually, I don't."

She raised an eyebrow. "Oh, really? Maybe this will jog your memory: Back in the second grade, you wet your pants on me, and I beat you up."

No. Way.

Sally Bean? This was not Sally Bean. How did she get so beautiful? No longer large. Completely un-mustachioed.

"Remember? We called you Pee Boy."

I heard a few giggles from the crowd.

Oh, please, not again. Deny, deny, deny.

"Nope, I don't remember."

"How could you not remember? What about Urine Trouble? The Slip Slide Kid?"

I shrugged. "No and no."

She grinned. "Oh, come on. How about my personal favorite: the Wee-Wee Wuss?"

Oh, man. I *hadn't* remembered that one.

Suddenly, I realized that everyone on the dock was listening . . . and laughing again. At me.

But I mostly noticed Sparky. He laughed the hardest. Now he looked like an *insane* munchkin. Or a demented ventriloquist dummy from a horror movie. I half expected smoke to start coming out of his eyes or ears or both.

I felt a rush of humiliation. I don't know if your life really flashes before your eyes when you die, but it definitely does when you're dying of embarrassment: Molly, the Butcher, Edwin, Sparky, Sally, Dad, Mom, Mom's heart, new life, old problems—they were all right there, bubbling up in me. All boiling like some kind of nasty Life Sucks soup.

My face got hot and I cried. A little.

I pulled my T-shirt up over my head and pressed it

227

against my face, hiding like that same wimpy turtle. I pretended to wipe off the canal scum, even though the shirt was totally soaked in it. I could see Mad Manny the Monkey through the fabric. Good old Manny. He always crashed, but he always came back.

I took a few deep breaths and poked my head out of the shirt again. I realized it might be hard to see someone's tears, anyway, if that someone also had toxic slime running down his cheeks.

The crowd was losing interest and moving away.

I looked at Sally Bean and thought of that day, way back when: the slide, the pee, the fist, the bloody nose, and the sand-caked crotch. I remembered my mom kissing me later and washing my pants and never talking about what happened, even though I knew she knew. She knew everything.

I thought about the years that followed, and how no one would let me live it down, even though Sally moved away not long after The Incident. And that now, after starting over at a new school, the nightmare had come screaming back, worse than ever. It was like a bad sci-fi movie. Sally Bean was some kind of cruel time-traveling-and-transforming beauty, sent on a mission from my past to screw up my future.

No matter what I did, Davis Delaware would be forever known as the Wee-Wee Wuss, the pathetic putz who had fallen into the pukiest canal ever, the doofus who was in love with Molly—a too-beautiful, too-smart girl who ended up hating him.

The Butchers had taken to the stage, and the amps were popping and squealing as they tuned up.

"How about some *real* music for a change?" Gerald laughed.

With that, they began blasting the kind of song that really gets a crowd revved up. Within minutes, everyone climbed aboard the barge and started dancing. Stephen Jablowski was right up front, howling like a happy coyote. Gerald would get back to the business of making everyone's life completely miserable as soon as break was over. But for now, he was a rock star.

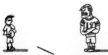

Sally Bean and I were alone on the dock. "Sorry I let that little secret out," she said.

I sighed. "Yeah, was that really necessary?"

"I think so. You never even apologized for the slide incident," she said.

"*I* was supposed to apologize to *you*?"

"You didn't get peed on."

She had a point. "I'm sorry. I guess it was as bad for you as it was for me."

"Worse," she said. "Plus, I had a serious puppy-love crush on you."

What the what?

"Wow," I said, pausing for a minute while it all sank in. "Punching me in the nose was a funny way of showing it."

"I wasn't going to. My plan changed after you did what you did. Getting peed on will change a girl's mind."

"Oh," I said. Maybe this actually made sense. What I'd remembered as an unprovoked attack was really just an act of self-defense. Who would have thought? "Okay, okay. So what are you doing here?"

Sally smiled. "Just transferred in. It was all about when my mom's new job started."

How on Earth had she changed so much? I could barely see her old face in this face. Blue eyes and dark hair, my favorite combination. Deepest dimples ever. She untangled a gloppy mess of canal gunk from the collar of my shirt. I noticed a big black earring dangling from her ear. It was shaped like a guitar pick.

"Wanna go for a walk?" she asked.

"Promise you won't punch me?"

"Promise you won't pee on me?"

That made me laugh. It's amazing what a cute girl can get away with saying to you.

It also sort of closed the book on the whole horrible slide episode. When something bad happens, people always say that someday you'll look back at it and laugh. All of a sudden, someday was here. We were both laughing, and that terrible shared memory not only seemed funny, it almost seemed good.

The Butchers were playing a famous band's famous song, the kind that every high school rock band plays. I had to admit, they sounded better than the Dweebs. A lot better. But everyone was cheering and dancing and freaking out, like somehow playing this same old song was a huge deal.

Sally rolled her eyes. "Lame," she said, walking away and gesturing for me to follow.

"Just a minute," I said.

I walked over and untied the barge from its moorings. One by one, I dropped the lines into the water.

Nobody noticed at first. They were too wrapped up in the party atmosphere. I sat down on the edge of the dock and put my feet on the side of the boat. I leaned back, took a deep breath, and strained against it with all my might. It moved a bit, but something was holding it back. Sally noticed some thick extension cords and unplugged them with a yank. The Butchers fell silent. The gangplank splashed into the water, and the barge drifted slowly away.

It took a second for the Butcher and all the others to figure out what had happened. Everyone shook their fists and yelled at us. Well, everyone except Edwin and Molly, who were both smiling and waving. I was glad about that. Molly even started blowing kisses, and I thought they were for me, but then I noticed Furry—old, bald Furry—sitting on a bench with Miss Danderbrook, blowing kisses back. He had a saxophone on his lap.

I gathered up what I could find of my notebooks as Sally and I walked over to the bench.

"One heck of a fund-raiser," said Danderbrook. "We made way more money than last year."

"Oh, good," I said wiping some canal muck off my face. "Hey, I'm sorry about that horrible drawing. I did it before I even knew you."

"That's okay." Danderbrook smiled. "Art isn't always pretty." Then she gave me a look. "Liberating that barge is a whole other question, though. You might be in deep bleep, if you know what I mean."

"Bleep yeah, I do," I said. "I hope Rigo goes easy on Edwin about defacing the locker, though. He was operating under the influence of a full-blown Molly obsession at the time."

Just then, my dad ran toward us from the parking lot. He was out of breath. "For heaven's sake, Davis, didn't I tell you to stay in bed? Why are you all wet? What happened to your *face*? Where's your guitar?"

"Oh, it's on that thing," I said, pointing to the barge. "Edwin'll bring it over. Which reminds me, I'm almost positive your sunglasses are at the bottom of the canal.

I'll figure out a way to pay for them." I watched Dad's eyes get wide, and I continued before he had a chance to say anything. "Hey, Dad, meet Sally, Furry, and Miss Danderbrook."

"Nice to meet you all," said Dad. Then he turned to me. "Let's go. You really need to sleep. I mean it."

"I know," I said. "But Sally and I are going to walk. I'll be home soon."

Dad gave me a look and sighed. Then he sat down on the bench between Furry and Miss Danderbrook. "How do you two know Davis?"

"We're old cronies from the barbershop," said Furry.

"Barbershop?" asked Dad.

"Davis is my poetry star," said Danderbrook.

"Poetry?"

I had a feeling Dad would have a lot of questions for me when I got home.

For now, Sally and I walked away.

"So, you're a poet," she said.

"Not really. I think I'm over that. Pretty much everyone hates me now, anyway. Except for maybe Molly and Edwin." *Molly and Edwin* sounded so wrong. But also kind of right. I was happy for them, but I knew my crush on Molly wouldn't instantly evaporate. Walking along with Sally helped. The fact that I was pretty sure she wasn't dating an ex-bed-wetting psycho-bully nut job like Gerald helped even more.

"Well, I for one don't hate you," she said with a smile. "At least not as much as I used to."

What a girl.

THE BEGINNING